Prison 268

Samantha Nicklaus

This is a work of fiction. Any resemblance to actual persons, living or dead, or actual events is purely coincidental.

Reviews can be left on Amazon.com and GoodReads.com

SamanthaNicklaus.com

Twitter.com/SamNicklaus

Facebook.com/AuthorSamNicklaus

Copyright © 2018 by Samantha Nicklaus

Logo by Ren Oliveira

All rights reserved. This book or any portion thereof may not be reproduced or used in any manner whatsoever without the express written permission of the author except for the use of brief quotations in a book review.

This book is dedicated to everyone who went through hell, then returned with water to help others.

Part One 1
Part Two 41
Part Three 93

Part One

It was silent, except for the sound of my shuffling feet and the soft clink of metal on metal.

My hands were shackled together. My feet were shackled, with another chain running up to my hands, connecting me to myself. I was in an orange jumpsuit, big and bright. My hair was in my face, but I couldn't reach up to move it. Two guards marched me down the empty hallway, each one holding one of my elbows, in case I tried to run. At the end of the hallway, a single door. They opened it and brought me inside.

The room was empty except for a single chair, placed in the center of the room, and a long table, where three men sat. They watched the guards walk me over to the chair. I sat down, and the guards moved so they were a few feet behind me. I couldn't see them, but I could feel them lurking.

I looked at the men at the table. The one on the left was skinny and young, like he had only had this job a day or two. The man in the middle was old. He looked a little bit like the Warden. Graying hair, gray suit. He was fatter, though, and looked more upset. The man on the right was tall and had little eyes, like a rat.

This is the best the Department of Prisoner Welfare and Psychology has to offer?

"Do you know why you're here?" the man in the middle asked me. The man on the left picked up his pen and started writing. I had no idea what he was writing; nothing had happened yet.

"I guess."

"Tell me."

"Because of the riot."

They all looked at me. Of course, it was because the Warden died. After Rabbit had killed him, it took all of five minutes for us to be taken in by the guards. We hadn't even barricaded the door or tried to run away. Everyone at the prison was re-arrested and re-charged. I had been innocent before. Now I was a criminal.

"Tell us what happened," the man on the right asked. The way he was looking at me bothered me. Like meat, like prey. I glared back at him.

"It was a riot, a lot happened," I said, looking him dead in the eyes. I had never seen another person look so annoyed in my entire life.

"We understand you were with the Warden at the time of his death," the man in the middle said. I didn't look away from the man on the right.

"Yes."

"Who killed him?"

"I don't know."

The man on the left sighed. "Heather, we need you to work with us. Who shot the Warden?"

"I don't know."

I remember it so perfectly, like the end scene in a movie, cut down into slow motion, playing over and over again. "Shoot him," I said, and Rabbit did. One shot to his forehead. It went straight through his head, his chair, and into the wall. He was dead in an instant.

"Heather," Rabbit said, holding the gun out for me. I took it. "Fire into the floor or something," he said. "We'll all have gunshot residue."

I held the gun in my hand, the first time I had ever held a gun. I was surprised by how heavy it was. I shot into the floor, by the

Warden's feet. He had made a puddle of blood from where Rabbit shot him in the knee earlier. I heard Pittman shoot too. Blood had never bothered me much before, but I expected to feel sick. When we burned people, I felt sick to my stomach. Like if I didn't really try to stay conscious, my body would just give up. But looking at the Warden, I felt a bizarre kind of peace. Like the chaos around me suddenly organized itself. It was still a pile of shit, but at least I could see what kind of shit it was.

Pittman handed his gun over to Socks, and he shot into the floor as well. "Listen," Pittman said, seriously. "They won't be able to know which one of us shot him. Either we all go down or none of us do."

Rabbit nodded. "They like to say that someone is talking, to get you to talk. Don't believe them."

Socks put the gun on the desk, and I set mine down next to his. "So, manslaughter or murder?" I asked. My innocence was not something I had missed. I had always assumed that to get into Prison 917, I must have committed a crime. To me, there was no other option. Knowing that I was actually innocent didn't change much, I guess. I was only innocent for a few seconds.

Within seconds of finally clearing your name, you order a man to death, I thought. The thought made me chuckle.

Pittman shrugged. "Honestly, they were never going to let us out anyway. Does it matter what the actual charge is?"

Socks laughed. "Isn't it funny, they finally end the death penalty nationally, but set up prisons like this? Then we shoot the guy who helped lock us up, and they can't do anything worse than keep us where we are."

Rabbit smiled. "They fucked themselves on this one."

I smiled. It was true. The second I was put into 917, I was as guilty as anyone else. I was there, and I was never getting out. Neither were they. It didn't make me feel like I belonged. It just made sense now. Now I knew *why*.

The door came flying open, and guards came pouring in. They weren't nice about arresting us. I got slammed into the filing cabinet so hard I cut my cheek and bruise my ribs. They twisted Sock's wrist to get him into cuffs until it popped and he screamed. Rabbit was thrown to the ground and practically sat on. Pittman was tasered, without question.

And now I was here. Being questioned by three men, who as far as I knew, were also responsible for me ending up in prison to begin with, asking me what happened.

"Listen," the man in the middle said. "I'm going to be honest with you, Heather, because you seem like a good kid. Your friend, the one you call Socks? He told us everything. We know it wasn't you. If you don't tell us what happened, we have to charge you too."

I cocked my head a little. "So what now, you send me to prison? You can't kill me for this. You can't kill the four of us for this. You want me to believe that before all of this, you were really just going to let me go home? I was stuck here either way." None of them said anything. "Did you put me in 917?"

"This isn't about that," the man in the middle said. "This is about the Warden's death."

"Why do you think he died?" I asked. "Because we were just so excited to see him? He—this entire department—fucked all of us over. And not just the four of us in that room."

"So this was a revenge killing?" the man on the right asked. His rat eyes pissed me off.

"Go fuck yourself," I said.

"Fine," the man in the middle said. "Fine. Don't tell us about the Warden. I have something else I need to talk to you about." I waited. "What do we do with the three hundred-something of you?"

That floored me. I expected us to be separated, send to different, but equally as shitty, prisons. "What?" I asked.

The man on the left took over. He had tired eyes. "We have decided that it is in the department's best interest to keep the remaining inmates from Prison 917 together, so they don't cause a disturbance anywhere else. That being said, we need to keep the inmates in a manageable location. Obviously, that wasn't possible in Prison 456. We would like your input."

"Why?" I asked. "You are accusing me of murder."

"We are *charging* you with murder," the man on the right corrected. I had the urge to jump over the table and kill him. To kill all of them.

"You were a leader in both prisons. You were innocent, up until recently. You are educated, and you know the mentality of those in the prison," the man on the left said. "We were never able to get a psychologist out to 456. We are relying on you."

"Not exclusively," the man in the middle added quickly. "But we will take your opinion into consideration."

I thought about what Rabbit said, about him being a fucked up person. Did I do something that was fucked up, or was I fucked up? I thought about the Warden, a bullet hole in his knee and in his head. About the peace that that brought me. I imagine men I had never met, sitting in their offices, sentencing kids to prisons like 917. I thought about them with bullet holes in their heads, too.

That's not justice, I told myself. *No*, I corrected. *Revenge and justice go together. Like peanut butter and jelly.*

I knew, deep down, that if I was free, I would want to see bullet holes in their heads. The people in the Department of Prisoner Welfare and Psychology. The people who sent me to 917, who sent all of us there. Noel, Brydie, Rabbit, Socks, Freddie, George, Pittman.

"You should put us back in 917," I said, almost shocking myself. "But with more space, actual housing, and supplies. We need access to food and water, always."

The man in the middle grunted. The two guards behind me, who I had forgotten about, stepped forward. I stood up, and they lead me out of the room.

I was expecting to go back into the cell I had come from. I had heard horror stories about solitary confinement. I guess they were a little nicer to me. Sure, the room was completely closed off, and I was alone, but I had five books and a deck of playing cards, so it wasn't all bad. Time alone, for the first week, was alright, I guess. I got to think things over, read a little. The second and third weeks were a lot harder.

I was expecting to go back there, that small little room, but I realized we weren't walking back the way we had come in. *Don't get excited*, I told myself. *You'll only be disappointed. You're going back there.*

We rounded a corner, went through a door, and, like magic; more cells. About ten of them. I could already hear Pittman talking.

The guards walked me past Socks and Rabbit. I got put in the fourth cell, right next to Pitt. They stopped talking, and we didn't say anything until the guards left us.

"Dude, the fuck!" Rabbit said with a smile. He stood there in his cell, wiggling like an excited puppy. "Look at us, back together again!"

"Probably for our execution," Socks said.

"Don't be such a pussy," Pittman snorted. "How you holding up, Red?"

"Did they talk to you guys yet?" I asked. They all said yes. "So I was the last one." I was trying to figure out what was going on. I hadn't expected to see anyone again, let alone my codefendants. "What did they ask you about?"

"What happened, why it happened," Rabbit said. "We didn't say anything."

"Of course, because nothing happened," Socks said. The cells were all bars, with no walls in between us. Down the line, I could see Socks snap, then point to his ear. We all nodded.

"Exactly," Rabbit said. "Exactly."

"So, what now?" Pittman asked.

"Trial? We wait for them to kill us?" I offered. No one seemed to like that answer, but we didn't have a lot of options.

"Have you gotten word from George?" Socks asked, quietly. Pittman shook his head.

"Guards here are stricter. Can't bribe any of them," he said, sadly. "He knows what this is, though. He knows."

We sat around. We talked. Wondered what happened to Delany, to Freddie. Rabbit sang until Pittman threatened to kill him. I had no idea how long we were in there, maybe five hours, six? Eventually, the door opened, and two guards came in. They went right up to Sock's cell and opened the door.

Socks stood up as they walked in, looking at them. "Give me your arm," one of them said. I watched Socks, through the bars, hold out his arm. Quickly, the guard grabbed him by the wrist, pulled out a needle, and stabbed him with it.

"Oh, you motherfucker," Sock yelled, pulling his arm back. He took two steps backward, then went down. One of the guards caught him, lowering him to the ground.

"Fuck," Rabbit said, looking around his cell.

"It's okay," I tried to tell him. "They're just moving us, it's okay."

"They just fucked killed Socks!" Pittman yelled, looking around his cell as well. I don't know why either of them thought they would magically find some way out now.

"Then why did they not let him hit his head?" I called out as they panicked. The guards had opened Rabbits door. He was backed against the corner. "Rabbit, stop!" I yelled at him. When they got close enough, he put his arms against the walls to hold himself up and used both feet to kick the guards.

They fell back, falling into each other. Rabbit hopped over them and headed for the door. One of the guards caught him by the ankle, bringing him crashing to the ground. A needle went into his ankle, and he didn't get up.

"Pitt, don't fight them," I begged as the guards got up. "It's going to be okay. You have to trust me. Please."

Pittman didn't look so sure. The guards were unlocking his door. "Are you sure?" he asked me.

"Yes," I lied.

Pittman held out his arm, and they stuck him. He went down, and it took both guards to make sure he didn't hurt himself. They came into my cell next. One stick in my arm and everything went black.

My head slammed against something cold and hard, and I was forced awake. As I blinked, trying to comprehend what happened, I could only see a green leather wall was in front of me. No, I realized, not a wall. It was the back of a bus seat. I looked around, and yes, I was on a bus. I had been chained to the metal that made up the side of the bus, and my head had smacked against the window.

I looked at the seat across from me. Cassidy. For once, I was happy to see that freak of nature. "Cassidy!" I whispered. "Cass!" She didn't move. That was fine, I didn't really want to have to hear her talk anyway.

I tried to stand up, but because my hands were chained, I could only make it halfway. I could see the person's head in front of me, just a mop of hair, but I couldn't tell who it was. I sat back down. Trees and grass flew past us as we moved, but nothing to give away where we were.

Maybe forty minutes had passed when the bus rolled down the road, then slowly came to a stop. I looked for a building or a fence, for anything really. Nothing but trees.

I heard the door open, and people step on to the bus. I could see her face. She had a mean looking face, but soft brown eyes. She looked around at us like she was counting, and we made eye contact.

"Heather?" she said quietly. I nodded.

She walked over to me, unlocking my hands from the chains. "I'm Lieutenant Gomez. I want you to come with me." My hands were completely free now, but that didn't seem to bother her. She smiled at me. The handcuffs on her belt stayed there.

She let me go first, walking down the bus aisle. I saw George, and Kyle, and Tiger. I was close to the front, so I didn't get to see a lot of people. I stepped off the bus, and there were more guards there. Freddie was standing there, next to a guard.

"Hey," she said, smiling, "you lived!"

"We're cockroach motherfuckers." I opened my mouth, but it was Rabbit's voice. Both of us looked, and there he was, walking towards us, with a guard in tow. I looked further behind him. There were more buses, it looked like four more. Other people were walking in behind Rabbit and his guard.

"What are we doing?" I asked Lieutenant Gomez.

She smiled at me a little bit. "We are showing you your new home. We want to make sure it will work for you."

"What?" I asked, but the Lieutenant didn't get to answer me. Rabbit called out Delany's name.

I whipped my head around so fast I was practically seeing stars. It was her, choppy hair and all. I ran at her, throwing my arms around her. "Oh, I was so worried about you," I gushed. Her arms didn't wrap around me. Behind her, Pittman and a guard walked over.

I heard her mumble "oh my god" to herself. I let go of her and looked her over. "Are you okay?" I asked.

"I'm fine," she snapped. I wanted to ask her what was going on, why she was being like that, but behind me, the Lieutenant asked us to start walking.

We walked for a little bit, following the road. I made sure to stay close to Delany, but it didn't seem like she cared much. Rabbit bounced around us as we walked. The road turned up ahead, and as we rounded the trees, we saw the fence. It could have been the exact same one from 917, but newer. Tall and buzzing. The Lieutenant grabbed her radio and mumbled into it, and the buzzing stopped. We got closer, and a small doorway appeared.

"We'll be taking this out, once you are all in there," Lieutenant Gomez said. She opened the door, and we all walked through.

It was the same set up as 917. The fence was about a mile away from the buildings. Even a mile away, I could see they were nicer than anything we had at 917. I could see roofs, real ones, siding, and shutters.

As we got closer, I could tell that I was right; it was much nicer than 917. Little houses, like the kinds those snobby hippies would buy, were lined up a grid pattern. They weren't big, maybe two rooms in the whole thing, but they were nice. Doors and windows, roofs. They were painted different colors, soft browns, and greens, a few of them looked vaguely pink, others light blue.

"Each house is about four hundred square feet. We have one for each of you, plus twenty more," Lieutenant Gomez said as we walked up to the first one. "Not that we are bringing more people in here."

Until she spoke, I hadn't realized that we had all been quiet the whole time. Even Rabbit. She tapped the side of the house. "Each one has running water and electricity. The main building there, it has solar panels on the roof that power everything here. Don't worry, there's a grate around them, so no one can throw rocks and break them."

We kept walking down the little path. It wasn't paved, but the grass had been cut so it was mostly dirt. "We have a house for everyone, like I said, this main building here we expect to be used as a town hall, and—" she waited as we rounded the corner.

Two white fences separated six cows, a lot of chickens, and four goats, from freshly plowed dirt that was just starting to show signs of green buds, with a row of trees behind it. It's where the cages would have been.

"A farm," Lieutenant Gomez finished.

Delany was the first of us to speak. "You think we won't fuck this up?" she said, almost laughing. She looked at Rabbit. "How many days until someone kills a cow?"

"Days?" Rabbit said, "I was thinking hours, Red."

Lieutenant Gomez lost her chipper attitude. "Listen. We realize that 917 was not the ideal situation. We had no control over that. We are trying to accommodate for your particular needs."

"So no guards?" Rabbit asked, one eyebrow raised. "We'll trash this place in a week, tops."

Lieutenant Gomez stayed strong. "It will be yours to trash. We would like to see you thrive here, but it's up to you." She glanced at me. "We have cameras to monitor you, in case there is an immediate need. Otherwise, you would be on your own."

"So, like a fire or something?" Pittman asked. The Lieutenant nodded.

"We brought you all here first to get approval. Are there any changes you think we could make? Any improvements?" She asked.

"Yeah. *Leave*," Delany said.

The Lieutenant ignored her. "Anything else?"

"All of the bathrooms work? Showers and everything?" Freddie asked. "Hot water?"

"All of them work," the Lieutenant said.

"Do I have to touch a cow?" Freddie asked. We all looked at her. "I'm not exactly farm friendly."

"So, you are afraid of chickens, or like?" Rabbit asked, trailing off.

"I just don't like things that hang out in their own poop," Freddie answered.

"And yet you lived in 917," Pittman said. Freddie pushed him. He barely moved.

The Lieutenant didn't say anything about our banter. In fact, she looked like a mom, just waiting for the kids to quiet down. I decided to help her out. "Honestly, nothing I can think of," I said. "You guys thought of everything."

"Sell out," Rabbit said.

"What do you want, then?" I asked him.

He thought for a second. "Drugs. Stripper poles. Guns would be nice. A racecar. Maybe—"

"Anything else?" The Lieutenant said, cutting him off. No one said anything. "Very well. We'll go get the others. Welcome to Prison

268." She turned like she was about to walk away, but Delany grabbed her arm.

For a second, I could feel the energy change. I liked the Lieutenant. She seemed nice. But in that half a second, I knew that if Delany tried to kill her, I wouldn't have stopped her.

Lieutenant Gomez wasn't fazed. She looked at Delany. Delany let go of her, slowly. "There are a thousand prisons," Delany said. "What happened to the kids who were here before us?"

It hadn't occurred to me before, but of course, Delany was right. Someone had to have been here before us. The Lieutenant looked scared now.

"They were moved," she said softly.

"Where?" Delany asked. When she didn't get an answer, she asked again. "Where are they?"

The Lieutenant didn't look at her. "They were put down."

"So much for reintroducing us," Pittman scoffed. "We were at a higher prison than them. If they are murdering the good kids—" his voice trailed off.

"And what makes you think they won't put us down next?" Delany asked Lieutenant Gomez. She didn't say anything, she just walked away from us.

"I saw George," I said quickly, before anyone else could speak. I didn't want to think of how many kids were murdered for our new home. "He was on the bus with me. He looked perfectly fine." Pittman closed his eyes for a second and let out a deep breath.

"Thank you," he said, reaching out and touching my shoulder.

"How sweet," Delany said. "Now, business. What's the game plan?" Apparently, the dead kids didn't bother her, either.

"Where were they keeping you guys?" Rabbit asked Freddie. "We got shoved off to solitary."

"We were back in the prison we all got sick in, only they wouldn't let us out anymore," Freddie said. "It was boring as shit."

"Tragic," Delany said, annoyed. "Now, what are we doing about this?"

"Doing about what?" Pittman asked.

Delany looked up at him. "This," she said, using both hands to motion at everything around us.

Rabbit looked around. "I don't know, Red. This doesn't look half bad, if we forget about the kids they killed. We can go back to being pieces of shit," he said. "That's all I really need. And maybe another murder spree. The last murder was fun, but it just wasn't enough, you know? What we really need is to kill all of them, I mean—"

"We'll have hot water," Freddie said, cutting Rabbit off. "Do you have any idea how—oh my god, you don't. Listen, I'm going to show you how to wash your hair, we can get that shit looking so *good*." Freddie reached out to touch Delany's hair. Delany slapped her hand away.

"And, much more importantly, we won't starve to death," I added. Rabbit pointed at me to agree. "This is what everyone wanted."

"Everyone?" Delany said. "Who died and made you queen?"

"The fact that you even know that expression is astounding," Freddie said.

"Delany, there is literally no way to improve on this place," I told her. "Do you really still want 917 that badly?"

"That is my home. Not this place, with these—" Delany motioned vaguely to the animals. "Things."

Pittman squinted his eyes and looked at her. "You don't know what a cow is, do you?"

"It doesn't matter!" Delany yelled. She looked like she was about to throw her hands up and stomp her feet she was so upset.

"Yeah, she has no idea what a cow is," Rabbit said, laughing. Delany looked like she was going to hit him, but instead, she turned and stormed off.

"Guys," I said, looking at the two of them

"What?" Rabbit said, chuckling. "I mean, it's a fucking *cow*."

I left them to follow after Delany. She had stormed off behind one of the houses nearby. I found her sitting in the grass, pulling up fistfuls of it. I sat down next to her. I didn't say anything for a bit, just let her throw grass onto my leg.

After a few fistfuls, she rest her head on my shoulder. "It's okay," I said softly. She picked up her head and looked at me. "I know that was your only home. You don't have to worry. This place won't be like those others."

"How do you know?" she asked me. She was only a few inches from my face, and I could see tears welling up in her eyes.

"Because," I said, not-so-confidently, "Those other places sucked, and we got out of them. If this place sucks, we'll get out of it too. But it won't. I won't let it."

She was quiet again and put her head back on my shoulder. "I heard you killed the Warden."

"Yeah, I did."

"Did you see our files?"

"Yeah."

"What did you do?"

I took in a deep breath. I hadn't considered the prospect of lying before. Socks would back up whatever I said. No one really trusts Rabbit. Pittman wouldn't care enough to argue. "Nothing," I said. "I didn't do anything."

"You shouldn't tell people that."

"I know."

We were quiet again. Delany picked two pieces of grass off of my leg and started to tie them into knots. I watched her for a few minutes. "What happened to you and Laura?"

"They picked us up climbing through the fence. Rabbit broke the thing that made it electric."

"That's what that bang was. You guys were okay?"

"Yeah. We were both okay." Delany picked up her head and moved away from me.

"What?" I asked her.

"Laura. She's fucking annoying sometimes." Delany threw her grass-knot mess away from her. "But she won't get killed."

I wanted to ask her what that meant when Pittman called out. We stood up and looked back the way we had come. They weren't there anymore. "To the front," Delany said, and I followed her. It was scary how similar the set up was to 917. We would have been sitting in Yellow, so we went back to the main road, against the town hall, and followed it back to the front gate. We didn't have the same archway anymore, though. It was just empty space. Pittman, Freddie, and Rabbit were standing there.

I followed their gaze. Three hundred-something kids were walking towards us, guards in tow.

Rabbit was beaming. "This is going to be a shit show," he said, then let out a loud laugh. "Ah, fuck me, this is going to be great."

I looked around. "We need a leader," I said as I thought it. They turned to look at me. "We can't go back to the groups."

"And why the fuck not?" Delany asked. Whatever emotional moment we had had before was over.

"We'll fight over the farm, the animals," I said quickly. The three hundred-something were getting closer. "We have to be unified. We couldn't do anything without trading for fucking water, we can't go back to that. People will die."

Pittman and Rabbit looked at each other. "I don't care about the groups," Pittman said. "They didn't mean much to me anyway." It occurred to me that they did mean a lot to Delany. I had already taken her from her home. Now I was trying to take away her identity.

Rabbit shrugged. "Yellow is with me no matter what. We are the only leaders left."

Freddie shrugged too. "I mean, I was just doing what I had to do. If I don't have to be responsible for anything and still get everything I need, I'm perfectly fine with that."

I looked at Delany. "One leader?" she asked. "That's fine." I could tell by the look on her face she thought it was going to be her, no question. I didn't like the idea, but I didn't say anything.

The Lieutenant was up in front. When she got to us, she told us to go into the town hall. "I want to welcome everyone," she said. Pittman started to walk through the crowd, looking for George. The four of us turned and walked into the town hall.

It was like the old town hall, but with no holes in the building. Without the constant threat of the building collapsing in on itself, this town hall was a lot more comforting. It was empty, with a stage against the back wall that was maybe four feet off the ground. We walked all the way up to it while the room filled up behind us. Rabbit jumped up and sat on the stage. The Lieutenant hopped up and put herself right up front.

When everyone had piled in, chatting and standing around, Lieutenant Gomez let out a long whistle, the kind that brings about dead silence. She smiled. "Welcome to Prison 268," she said. "Now, we know you have had bad experiences in the past. Prison 268 is as close as we can get to putting you back in 917. We model it after how you had set up in 917. This town hall is the center, with the houses you saw in a circle around it. Instead of cages, we have a farm where you can grow food and care for the animals."

She took a second to look around the room. "Listen, I'm a cop, not anyone important enough to call the shots here. I know how hard your lives have been because of the DPWP. I hope this works out for you. I really do. We want you all to be happy."

"That sounds like a radio station," Freddie whispered to me.

Still, in dead silence, Lieutenant Gomez hopped off the stage. The crowd parted to let her through. Rabbit jumped up to take her place right way. Without hesitating, Delany and I followed him.

"Hey," Rabbit said, a beaming smile. "So happy we're all back together again."

"Shut up, Rabbit," Delany said, then more loudly, "We need a leader."

"One leader," I added. "The groups didn't work before."

"I don't know, maybe—" Rabbit started to say. I cut him off.

"You killed Cye because she didn't agree with you and we burned people alive," I reminded him. "That is not what I would call functional."

"Says you," Rabbit snapped. "We had fun."

"We can have fun here," I said. "With one, universal leader. We don't need six of them, plus seconds. It's pointless."

Rabbit glared at me. "Fine. I nominate myself as leader." Some people started to cheer—it wasn't hard to tell they were all Yellows. "I started the riot that got us here, I deserve to lead."

I waited for Delany to say something, and she did. "You are both complete idiots," she snapped. "You," she said, pointing to me, "got us out of 917, where we were perfectly fine. And you," she pointed to Rabbit, "got thirteen people killed in that riot."

"How many people did you burn to death?" Rabbit asked her. "Way more than thirteen. They fought and died for us to escape."

"Which we *didn't do*," Delany yelled. "I nominate myself."

While the two of them were glaring at each other, I looked back at the crowd. "Anyone else want to nominate themselves? Or someone else?" No one spoke up. "Alright, ugh, I guess we should hold a vote now then." I looked around and no one was objecting. "Give each person two minutes to make their case, then we'll vote."

"Why do you get to make the rules?" Rabbit asked.

"Do you want to do this differently?" I said.

"No, but why did you get to say it?"

Delany pushed in front of him. "I'm going first." Rabbit went to step in front of her, but I grabbed his arm and pulled him to the side with me. Delany took the center of the stage, ready to speak.

"I was born in 917," she said. "No one knew that place better than me. I ran Red for years. You all know me. You know that I'm a good leader, a strong leader. I had nothing to do with us getting out of 917, and I had nothing to do with us getting out of 456. I'm not here to rock the boat. I'm not here to bother you. You just do your thing, and I'll do mine. Nothing to it."

There was cheering, and from what I could tell, it wasn't only Red. Rabbit wiggled away from me. "You done?" he asked, and she stepped out of the way. "I got us out of that hellhole Heather got us into," he said, jabbing his thumb in my direction. "I fought the guards, right along with you guys. I might not have led Yellow for that long, but I'm willing to fight for us. Delany? What has she done for you? Sat around and slept with her girlfriend. I was out there, getting shit done. Yeah, this place seems great now, but when shit hits the fan, who do you want? Me, who can handle it, or Delany, who will sit around?"

More cheers, not just from Yellow this time. I wasn't really listening to Rabbit though, I was trying to figure out how to do the voting. I figured secret ballots would be best, but just standing on one side or the other seemed faster and—

Everyone was looking at me. Even Rabbit and Delany. "What?" I asked Delany.

"It's your turn, idiot."

I hadn't nominated myself, and no one else had. I didn't know what to say. "Alright," I said, taking a few steps over so I was in the middle of the stage.

"I was a second in Red, and I helped Delany. I learned a lot from her," I said. I didn't really know how to make a case for myself. I realized I probably didn't have to; I just had to make a case against them. "Rabbit is a drug addict," I said, a little more confident. "Who used drugs to gain favors. Delany is a good leader, but she doesn't know about the world we're in now. In 917, she was perfect. We don't have time for her to adapt to cows and bell peppers. We need someone now.

"I know a lot of you hate me for getting us kicked out of 917, and I know that I didn't exactly help get us out of 456. But I know you guys realize that having food and water is big. Having a roof over your head is big. We were kicked out of 917, by and large, because of that storm that destroyed Red. Nine people died in that storm. There was nothing we could have done about it. Here, we don't have that problem. You aren't going to be crushed to death by your roof, or go hungry because a drunk Yellow pissed on a Green's garden. You don't have to negotiate with Blue for water.

"All we have to do here is get along. I don't want to be the leader so we can go back to the barter system and fighting. I just want to live my life," I finished.

There was mild cheering, nothing more than Delany or Rabbit had gotten. "So, how are we doing voting?" Delany asked me.

I looked around the room. "Alright," I said. "Everyone who wants Rabbit, come over here." I pointed up towards the stage, to the right. "Delany, over here." I pointed to the left side of the room. "And me, I guess back there."

"We need someone to count, who won't fuck it up," Rabbit said.

As everyone shuffled around the room, we threw out suggestions. "Cassidy?" I said. For once, she might be good for something.

Delany shook her head. "I punched her in the mouth once."

"Drake?" Rabbit suggested.

"The Green or the Purple?" Delany asked.

"Purple."

"I punched him, too."

"Green, then."

"Yeah, kicked him in the dick."

"What is wrong with you?" I asked her, and she shrugged. "What about Pitt? He likes all three of us."

"No, he knows I'm a dipshit," Rabbit said. "Plus, I stole from him once."

"And I punched him once," Delany added.

"I swear to god," I said. "George?"

The looked at each other. "I haven't hit him," Delany said.

"I haven't stolen from him. Green doesn't have a player in this. I'm good with it."

We turned back to face the room. "George?" I called. Like, eight people called back. "Green George." Still, two people. "Pitt's husband."

"I'm over here!" he said, not yet standing with a side.

"Perfect, come here," I said, waving him over. He ran right up to us. "We need you to count the number of people in each group. Fairly. No bias, and no lying."

George nodded. "Of course."

Even without counting, we could start to see how things were playing out. Delany and I looked about tied, and Rabbit's side was lacking. I heard Rabbit mumble about how it was bullshit while the last of the people wandered into place.

When everyone was in place, George went around counting. Delany said we had lost thirteen people in the riot. We lost two when we all got sick. Meaning we should be at about three hundred sixty-seven now.

George announced each group as he was done counting them. "Ninety for Rabbit," he announced. Rabbit's side cheered, even though they were clearly the losers.

He counted Delany's. "One hundred and twenty-six!" Her side cheered as well.

He counted mine. It felt like it was taking forever. "You won," Delany said. "Congrats. Don't fuck it up."

Before I could say anything, George called out my number. "One hundred and forty-five!"

Fuck. I closed my eyes. *Fuck.* Sure, I didn't want Delany or Rabbit in charge, but I didn't want that responsibility either. Mostly because I knew it came with the task of trying to manage Delany and Rabbit. I did not want to be responsible for that.

I opened my eyes, and the entire room was staring at me in completely and utter silence. *Fuck. I have to do something.* "Ugh, alright, let's get housing squared away," I said, not even because I cared, but I wanted everyone to get away from me for ten minutes.

I wasn't sure if I could trust them to just go find a house for themselves, or if they would try to kill each other over them. I decided that I didn't honestly care if they fought over it. "Alright, here's what we're going to do," I said, loudly. "Same set up as 917. If you were in Red, take a house to the right of the entrance, then Orange, then Yellow—you get the deal."

"What about food?" Someone yelled out.

"Get houses first," I said quickly. "We'll do food next. At sundown." I had no fucking idea where the sun was, or what time it was. Sundown seemed like a good marker, though.

Some people took off running, trying to get the best house. They were all the same, and the people who realized that casually walked away. Rabbit and Delany stood with me, watching everyone leave. "You sure you're up for this?" Delany asked me.

"No," I said, honestly.

"I'll do it," Rabbit offered quickly, hopping a little.

"No," Delany and I said at the same time. "I'd rather Delany than you," I added. Delany raised an eyebrow. "Don't get excited, I'm not giving the job up just yet."

"If I don't get to be the boss, I'm going to go grab a house," Rabbit said, hopping off the stage. "See ya."

Delany and I watched him go. "What's the plan here?" she asked me.

I sighed. "Houses now, then we'll figure out the food situation. We all have running water. Tomorrow, I guess, assign jobs. Someone has to take care of the animals and the food."

"Green and Orange can do food, Purple and Blue can do animals," Delany suggested. "Red and Yellow are doing to need something, though. We only have like ten Pinks left, but there's your police force."

I looked at Delany. I was so used to her being in charge, I almost just told her yes right away. But it wasn't a democracy. Well, I guess it was, but she didn't get a direct say. "I'll think it over," I said. "I don't know if I want 'police' around."

"You have to have something," Delany said. "That was the whole point of having leaders for the groups, to solve fights. There are going to be fights." She did have a point there. "I'm going to go find a house."

"Laura probably got you guys one," I said. I didn't want her to leave. Not yet.

Delany nodded. "I'll grab my own. Seems like we have plenty to spare." She jumped down off the stage. I watched her walk the whole way out, leaving me all alone.

Fuck.

I grabbed a house by the entrance. Actually, it was the first house, right by the empty field. I could just barely see the road we walked in on. It was a light brown house, with red shutters and a red front door.

I hadn't really thought about the inside of the houses. I opened the front door and was hit with the smell of fresh paint. It was a little overbearing. I was standing in a little living room—one couch and one chair, a coffee table, and a little bookshelf. There were about fifteen books on it, all classic looking books, like the stuff I had to read in high school. There was a little kitchen as well.

I walked over and ran the sink. It sputtered for a moment, but clear, cold water came out. I opened the fridge. It had an empty plastic pitcher in it, but nothing else. The stove next to it was electric. I clicked on the burners, holding my hand over them to make sure they actually got hot and then flipped them back off.

"We're going to need a maintenance team," I said to myself. "This shit is going to break eventually." I had Red and Yellow left to pick from. *Red.*

There was a little hallway next to the kitchen. The door on the right opened up to a little bathroom. I ran the sink and the tub, flushed the toilet. Everything worked. I looked at myself in the mirror.

I wanted to say I didn't recognize myself, that my time in prison had changed my appearance. But it hadn't. I looked a little older. I lost some weight in my cheeks. But anyone who had known me before would still recognize me. Same blonde-ish hair, same hazel eyes. I felt like a completely different person, but I looked exactly the same. Something about that set my teeth on edge, and I walked out of the bathroom.

The bedroom was simple—a bed and a dresser, which had a few shirts in it. I walked back out, closing the door behind me. Standing in the living room, I looked around again.

The smell of paint was becoming too much, and I went to the windows and pushed the shutters open. The windows didn't have any glass in them—which would have been nice, but I was happy to avoid the possible weapon. A breeze ran through the little house, bringing in fresh air.

I sat down on the couch.

Alright, what do I need to do? I thought. *Food. Jobs.* I looked around, looking for another person. I wanted Delany, or Pitt, or Socks. Someone.

I got up and went to the front door, throwing it open. It wasn't loud outside like it was at the other prison. I could hear people talking, and laughing, but there was a new calmness. Everything was a bit more spread out, the houses weren't as close together. We were in our own little suburb now.

I started walking through New Red, along the town hall's brick wall. I walked until I got to the farm, and four kids were in there with the animals, chasing the chickens.

"Hey!" I yelled, already climbing over the fence. "Get the fuck out!"

Luckily, that was enough to scare them off. They hopped over the other side of the fence and didn't look back. The chickens settled down and went back to doing whatever chickens do. I stood in the center of the enclosure.

"You okay?"

It was Socks. I turned around and saw him leaning on the fence. I walked over. "I have no fucking idea how to take care of a goat," I said, feeling my throat get hot. *We are* not *going to cry*, I ordered myself. *No.*

Socks smiled. "We'll figure it out."

"I had to chase some kids off who were fucking with the chickens."

"Well, people are going to mess with—wait, fucking with, or *fucking* with?" Socks asked, then laughed at what must have been a horrified look on my face. "Look, don't worry so much. We're going to fuck this up. Not you, *we*. Everyone. Once you acknowledge that this is going to be a fucking shit show, it'll be alright."

"But I don't want it to be a fucking shit show," I said, my voice catching. If Socks noticed I was starting to cry, he didn't say anything.

"When I was like, seven or eight, my uncle got this brand new car, right? This shiny little thing, all fancy heated seats and shit. My family isn't big with money, so this was a huge deal. He had the car like a week and we went out to dinner, my whole family. My mom and I are riding back with him in this car, and he's talking to my mom about how much he loves it, right? Just going on and on. I'm back there with gum in my mouth, just looking out the window. But I'm a stupid fucking kid, and the gum comes out of my mouth, right onto this brand new seat.

"So I panic, trying to pull it up, but it's just getting stringy and making it worse. So I start crying right away because I know my mom and uncle are going to kill each other trying to decide who gets to kick my ass," Socks said, pausing to laugh.

"They're asking me what's wrong, and I tell them what happened. My mom starts going on and on about how I don't pay attention and I'm going to get my ass beat. We pull up to my house, and me and my mom get out of the car. She grabs me by the back of the neck, ready to drag me into the house.

"My uncle, he's still in the car. He looks out the window at us, and he picks up one of those to-go cups from the restaurant, full of soda. He's looking straight at us, and it's so weird my mom's stopped screaming. He takes the lid off and pours like half of the cup right onto the passenger seat.

"Now, I don't know what the fuck to say, right? So he looks at us and goes 'It's just stuff, man. It's not going to be new forever.' That's what this is. No matter what, there's going to be soda on the seat eventually, no matter how careful you are. Don't stress about the gum."

"So your uncle ruined his car because it was going to get ruined eventually anyway?" I asked.

Socks nodded his head. "Pretty much."

I looked at him. "I'm not sure that helped."

Socks nodded a few times. "Yeah, I'm not so good with life-altering advice."

We stood there for a second, hanging on the fence. Behind me, chickens clucked. "What about some straightforward advice?" I asked him.

"Shoot."

"Having a police force, to watch over things. Good or bad?"

Socks thought for a second. "General police? Bad. But we're going to need to protect the food. What are you thinking, same deal as 917? Pinks guard shit?" I nodded. "I'd do that," he said.

I looked back behind me, at the animals. *Fucking animals.* "Would you mind going to track down Pitt for me?"

Socks nodded. "You good here, by yourself?"

I thought for a second. "Yeah, yeah I'm good."

I watched Socks until he disappeared around the corner. It was still mid-afternoon, the sun was bright and high. I wanted it to be dark. I wanted for today to be done with. Tomorrow, after I slept, I'm sure I could handle this. But right now, it was just too much.

I stood there, leaning on the fence, waiting. Pitt, at least, I knew I could count on. He would handle this so I could go figure out the food situation. If there was even one to figure out. The Lieutenant had said that food was covered, but nothing seemed ready yet. Killing the animals seemed stupid, and none of the plants had anything to harvest. They probably wouldn't for a few days. I should have asked her about that.

I should have kept my mouth shut. Let Delany lead. She would know what she's doing. She wouldn't be standing in a field with cow shit waiting for help.

Pittman rounded the corner, George and Socks in tow. I could physically feel a weight lift off my shoulders. "Hey," George said, holding out his hand. I climbed over the fence, holding his hand to steady myself. Once I was safely on my feet, he put his arms around me.

"Thank you, for looking out for him," he said in my ear.

"Thank you for looking out for me," I said back. He let me go, and Pitt nodded at the farm.

"You want me to stay here?" he asked.

"Yeah, you and whoever you need to help. I already had to chase a few kids away," I said, looking back. "We can't have them kill the animals. Milk, cheese, eggs—it's more important. And make sure no one fucks with the plants, either."

George looked up at Pitt. "Is it just me, or does she curse more now?"

Pittman put a hand on my shoulder. "You got it, boss."

"Thanks," I said, and started to walk away. "Oh, and find people to work shifts, day and night. Pinks, if you can."

"I thought we didn't have groups anymore," Pitt called back to me.

"Fine, find me some big scary fuckers," I yelled back, and he smiled.

Socks followed after me. "What do you need me to do?" he asked. I liked Socks, but I needed a minute alone.

"You can help Pitt round up some Pinks," I said. He looked at me. "I just need to figure out what's going on, what I want to do next."

"Talk to me about it."

I stopped in the middle of the road. He stopped too. "Right," he said with a sad nod. I don't know what he was thinking. "I'll go help Pitt." I could have argued with him, told him that I really did just need a minute alone to think, but I didn't care enough to. I had things to do.

With everyone still running around outside, the town hall was empty. I walked in, letting the cool air take me in. I took in a deep breath, looking around. *This is what 917 could have been*, I thought. *Fuck, even if they had just cleaned out the machinery.*

Wait, am *I cursing more?*

I walked over to the stage and hopped up, looking back at the empty room for a second. Empty. Completely empty. I was on my own, here. No guards, no Warden, no groups. Just me.

No time for a pity party, I thought. *Time to work.*

I turned around. There was a table, pushed up against the wall. A couple of chairs. A blanket draped over something. I walked over and pulled it off.

A door.

The handle was carved into the door, one of those little metal laches you had to hook your finger around and pull on. It was so tightly built into the wall that if you didn't notice the dip for the little handle, it would just look like more wall. I opened the door.

A supply room.

I looked behind me. Town hall was still empty. I walked through the doorway, letting the door close behind me.

There was food. A *lot* of food. I picked up one of the packages. Freeze-dried eggs. Good for up to ten years. *Ten years*, I thought. I hadn't thought about being here for ten years. For the rest of my life.

I will be doing this for the rest of my life. I won't go to college, have a career, get married, have kids. I'll be here. In this prison. Looking at freeze dried eggs.

Suddenly, I felt like throwing up. I could feel it, in the back of my throat. Without thinking, I sat on the floor. *It's okay*, I told myself. *This is fine. We're going to be fine. It's okay. You're okay.* My heart was beating so loud I could hear it echoing around in my head. My whole body was shaking with the force of it.

Deep breath. Deep breath. We're okay. We're okay. One day at a time.

I put down the freeze dried eggs in my hand and looked around the room. Bottled water. A pile of first aid kits. Five toolboxes. Paper, pens. Three stoves. Piping. A flare gun.

As I looked around, the nausea started to go away. *Just think about right now. What do we need right* now?

I need to get up. *Someone will come in here soon. No one should know about this.*

I stood up, using some of the shelving to pull myself to my feet. I turned around to head out, and above the door, hanging on a nail, was a key on a string. I took it and put it around my neck, tucking the key under my shirt.

I grabbed a box of freeze-dried beef stew and opened the door wider. I grabbed another box, and another, and another. *Four boxes should be good.* I went and took the key from my neck, locking the door. I put the blanket back over the nail, hiding the door, and put the key back around my neck.

I closed my eyes.

I should keep this to myself. If I tell anyone, we'll blow through supplies too quickly. Sure, the Lieutenant said they would help us, but what if they didn't? What if they had said the same thing when they sent kids to 917? Or the kids they killed to give us this place? We have to save that, for emergencies.

"You figure out food yet?"

I opened my eyes. Laura. And Delany. I hadn't heard them walk in.

They walked in with a handful of other people, all Reds. "Hey," I said, hoping no one noticed my voice shaking, "Yeah, they left us a box of freeze-dried food."

"Ew," Laura said. She grabbed Delany's hand. "Can't we find something else?"

"There's nothing else, baby," Delany said. "Pitt is real up-tight about that farm."

At least that went right, I thought. "It doesn't look that bad. Beef stew."

Laura scrunched up her nose. "I'm a vegetarian."

"Sorry," I said. "Is everyone else headed in?"

Delany shrugged. I looked at another Red, Bob. "Hey, would you mind spreading the word that I got food step up in here?"

"Sure thing," he said. "Just save me some."

Delany held out her hand, and I got one of the packages and handed it to her. "What the fuck is this?" she asked, shaking it. "It sounds like sand."

Laura took it out of her hands. "Beef stew, with carrots, blah blah blah, add water—wait, that's it? Just add water and this will magically become beef stew?" She looked up at me.

"It's just for today," I said. "We'll have the farm up and running. You can go back to not eating meat."

Laura handed it back to Delany. "This sucks."

"Well, it is prison, Laura," Delany said. She shook the package again. "Ugh." She put out her hand, and I handed her another. "Come on, let's go."

Delany and Laura left together. The other Reds started to line up, and I sat down on the stage, handing them packages of freeze-dried shit. I watched Delany and Laura leave together, and I wanted to leave, too. I wanted to read Delany packaging she couldn't read, to show her how to turn on a stove, how to heat up water. I wanted to see her face when she tried beef stew. I wondered if she would like it.

More and more people came into the town hall, and I was busy passing out packages of beef stew. It felt like it took six hours. Socks was one of the last people to come in.

"Hey," I said when it was his turn. "You picking up for Pitt and George too?" He nodded, and I handed him three packages.

"What are you doing after this?" he asked me.

"Ugh," I said, looking around. "I hadn't thought about it. I guess going home, eating?"

"You're the house on the end, right? Right by the entrance, in Red?" he asked.

"Yeah, why?"

"Can I stop by later? I want to talk to you."

"Ugh, yeah, sure."

Whatever Socks wanted, I didn't have time to worry about it. I finished passing out food. I had no idea what to do with the boxes, so I stacked them together and took them back to my house, figuring I could find a use for them later.

I went through my cabinets until I found a pot. It didn't take long; they cabinets were practically empty. I put water in it and set it on the stove. I wandered around the living room, waiting for it to boil.

My side window looked out towards the entrance, then into Pink. The sun was just starting to set, but there weren't any lights on in Pink. Hopefully, that meant they were with Pittman, watching over my farm.

There was a knock at the door, and I answered it. Socks was standing there, looking oddly uncomfortable. "Hey," I said. "I was just about to eat."

"Do you want me to come back?" he asked, already turning to head out.

"No, no, stay," I said. "I can do both." Behind me, I heard the water start to boil. "Come on."

I went and took the pot off the stove, poured the powder into a bowl, and added water. "It looks worse than it tastes," Socks warned me.

"Thanks. So, what's up?" I asked, stirring the water and powder together.

"I just—" Socks started. "Listen, you're in charge now, and I think that's great. I mean, I voted for you. I think you can do a really good job here. You're smart, and you care, and you aren't a total shit head."

"Just kind of a shit head?" I asked. I tasted some of the beef stew. It could have been a lot worse. Oddly salty.

"You get my point. I just wanted to say, Delany and Rabbit—they're the angel and the devil on your shoulder. Don't listen to them too much. They're only in this for themselves."

"Huh," I said, thinking for a second. "Who's the angel and who's the devil?"

"It's an expression," Socks said, looking at bit annoyed. "Honestly, I think both those idiots are devils, but that's not the point. You have me, Pitt, George—were on your side. They aren't."

I wasn't sure I agreed with him. "Delany's taken care of me," I said. "She's a bit fucked up, but she does care about me. And Rabbit, he's—he cares in his own way. I'm not saying I trust them with my life, but I don't think they're out to get me. And Rabbit and I sort of killed a guy together."

"I think that means a lot more to you than it does him," Socks said. "He's killed like four people. More, if you include overdoses."

"Still though," I said.

Socks nodded. "That's fine. I just wanted to let you know who has your back."

"Thank you," I said. "This isn't going to be a one-man show. I'm going to need help."

"Anything you need," Socks assured me.

"Oh, actually," I said, "I did want to talk to Delany. Do you know what house she's in?" Socks looked at me. "I have to make a list of people so I can assign jobs. If you know someone who knows the people here better, I'm all ears."

"She's like five houses down, two roads up," he said. "I'm out for the night. I'm right on the edge of Orange, by the front, if you need anything."

He left, and probably closed the door a little harder than he had to. I finished my stew and put the bowl in the sink. I looked around the living room. I needed a pen and paper. The side table next to the couch had a little drawer. I opened it and found a little notepad and a few pens.

I was suddenly hit with the memory of Delany's little black book, with the names of Red's who had died. I wonder where it was now. Probably in some psychologist drawer. I didn't like that idea.

I grabbed my things and headed to Delany's.

"What do you want?" she asked when I knocked on the door. I could see Laura laying on the couch behind her.

"I need your help with something," I said. "I have to set up jobs for everyone."

Delany smirked, for half a second. "And you need to know who's good for what."

"Yeah."

"Come in."

With Laura taking up the whole couch, I stood there for a second. Delany didn't close the door. "Laura, go home for a bit," she ordered. Laura looked up at her like she was going to argue, but put on her shoes and left.

"You run a tight ship," I said, sitting down on the couch.

"What?"

"You're a hard-ass," I corrected, pulling the coffee table closer to me.

"Is that news to you?" She sat down next to me. "Let's start with Pink, that's easy."

We went through every person in the prison. Delany knew every one of them. I thought we would have to go through the list a few times, figure out who we were missing. She got every person's name in one go, like she had spent years memorizing it. Which, I guess, she had.

"My graduating class was two hundred kids and I couldn't name all of them," I said to myself. "You've got a good memory."

Delany shrugged. "Have to remember who not to piss off, you pissed you off, and who you can get back at."

I looked down at my list. "You didn't help pick jobs based on revenge, did you?"

Delany laughed. "If I did, I would have told you to have Rabbit shoving shit."

"I don't—" I stopped.

"For Angel," Delany said, cutting me off. "I really should have killed him."

"Why didn't you?" I asked. This was pushing, even for Delany.

She shrugged. "I needed him alive. Yellow has a lot of people, I needed to make sure they were on my side. Rabbit is loyal, if nothing else. Hell, it took him four months to actually kill her. He didn't want to upset me."

"You guys actually are friends, huh?"

"I guess. I guess he's like the brother I never wanted. Still don't want."

Before Delany could even say it, I promised her I wouldn't tell him she said that. "I'll get out of your hair. Thanks for your help." I stood up, and Delany did as well.

"You want some advice? Don't start killing people."

I knew she was talking about the burnings. "I won't."

"You're going to want to," she told me. "Don't."

Part Two

I woke up bright and early to the sound of birds chirping. I got out of my bed, washed the dishes, took a shower. Normal person things. In the dresser, I found a range of clothes, all different sizes. I got a big shirt and used a hair tie from the bathroom to tie it shorter. Clean hair, clean clothes. It made all the difference.

I opened my front door and saw George, fist up. "Hey," he said, lowering his hand. "I was about to knock."

"What's up?" I asked, "Is the farm okay?"

"Peachy," he said. "I was just going to ask if you figured out jobs for everyone."

"Yeah, why?"

"What do you have me doing?"

"You're taking care of the farm. In charge of it, actually," I said. "Why, did you want something else?"

George smiled. "No, that's exactly what I wanted. When are you giving out assignments?"

"Once I get everyone together," I said. "Actually, if you want to help me run around and tell people to get to the town hall, that would be great."

"Of course. I'll take Green through Pink." George skipped off. Literally, skipped. *At least someone is having a good time.*

I went around to Red, Orange, and Yellow, telling everyone who was awake to head to town hall. I got to maybe a third of the people. I couldn't really blame anyone for sleeping in. I wouldn't have been awake if it wasn't for those birds.

This new prison was so similar to 917, but it felt off. Like visiting your elementary school. It's still the same, but somehow not quite as you remembered it. I wasn't used to having to walk back to the front of the prison to get in to town hall, but that was one of the tradeoffs with having a building that didn't have holes in the sides of it. I walked back to the front and found about a hundred people already waiting for me.

I made my way through the crowd while everyone talked. It was like a school assembly. Only instead of pretending to listen to some teacher, I had to *be* the teacher. I went and took my place on the stage, flipping through my papers a few times before I whistled to get everyone's attention.

"I think the easiest way to do this is to form a line," I said, pointing to the front of the stage. "You tell me your name, I'll tell you your job. Sound good?" It wasn't really a question, but some people started to complain about having jobs.

"Hey, this prison isn't going to run itself," I said. "Line up."

By the time everyone woke up and found their way over to me, it was getting late. I probably spent five hours sitting there, assigning jobs. Some people argued, but mostly they just asked questions. Why do I have to work? What happens if I don't show up? Who is in charge of me? Why do I have to do that? That kind of stuff. It didn't bother me at first. By the two hundredth person, I understood why Delany just yelled at people.

When I finally got out of there, I headed straight over to the farm. Pittman was still there, sitting on the fence. "Careful, if you break that, we're fucked," I told him. I hopped up and sat next to him.

"Nah, they planned for big fuckers like me," he said. "How was job assignments?" I looked at him. "That bad, huh? Who knew getting convicts to work would be so hard."

"I figured if they were working for things like their own fucking food they would be a little better about it," I said with a sigh. "Why is everyone such a pain in the ass?"

Pittman laughed. "I don't know, kid. I don't know."

We sat there for a little bit, just watching. Pittman had a Pink on each corner of the fence, and one in with the animals and the plants. Another two walked around down by the trees. "Any trouble yet?" I asked him.

"Yet?" He said with a raised eyebrow. "It's Pink. No one is going to cause any trouble with us."

"Can I get that in writing?" I asked. "We used all that freeze-dried shit yesterday. If this doesn't give us something, we're fucked."

"We're used to being fucked," Pittman reminded me. "Not eating for a day or two won't kill any of us."

"Hey," George said from behind us. We both turned to look at him. "How's it going?"

"Just the man I wanted to see," I said, moving so I was facing his way on the fence. "We got anything with the farm? How long until we have some food?"

"Well," George said in a way that told me I was not going to like what he was about to say. "Good news is, there will be enough produce to keep us going. Plenty for everyone. That, plus the milk, eggs, and cheese—butter if we can figure out a good way to do it—we'll be set."

"Bad news?" I asked.

"Bad news, we're about two weeks out from that. At least."

I sighed. "Two weeks? Couldn't they have fucking kept us for two more weeks? Fuck!" I looked straight up at the perfect blue sky. That wasn't helping my mood.

"I know," George said. "I can scrape by, maybe, but it's not going to be enough for everyone. And realistically, it would be better for the plants if we waited."

"Less than twenty-four hours into this shit," Pittman said. "God bless you, Red."

I looked at George. "What do you got?"

"Potatoes, mostly. They're small right now, but edible."

"What else?"

"Some apples, I guess, but those need at least four days to be any good. Again, better if we wait."

I thought for a second. I thought if I could cover the basics, we would be set. We had water and housing. All we needed was food. *How the fuck do I manage that?* The idea popped into my head so suddenly, I barely even realized what I was doing when I hopped down off the fence. "I'll let you know," I said to George.

"Where are you going?" Pittman asked me.

"We need shit," I said. "And I know someone who is good at getting shit."

◆

Rabbit was beaming at me. "So you need my help?"

He picked a house dead center in Yellow, which didn't surprise me. "Yes, I do," I said. He leaned in the doorway.

"I missed this," he said. "For a second there, it seemed like our little girl was all grown up."

"Shut up."

"Ah, you wound me," Rabbit said, putting a hand to his chest. "Come on, get in."

I went and looked around. His house was set up just like mine, only messier. He had managed to take everything out of every drawer and cabinet and scatter it about the house. I went to the couch, straightened the couch cushions, and sat down. "Do you have a set up already?"

Rabbit threw himself into the chair next to me. It slid. "No, but I have a lead."

"A lead?"

"Yeah, my brother found a guard who has some gambling debt. He's going to talk to him to see what we can do about getting me some treats."

"You have a brother?" I asked. "You've never mentioned him before."

"Paranoid motherfucker," Rabbit said, shaking his head. "I end up in jail, he thinks everyone is out to get him." Rabbit chuckled. "Actually, knowing about The Department of Kiss My Ass, he might be right."

"How do you talk to him?" I asked. I had never really thought about how people got things into 917. That was one of the things over my head, something I didn't have time to concern myself with. But now, I was curious.

"Long story," Rabbit said, waving his hand. "Don't worry about it. What do you need in?"

I hadn't really gotten that far. "Whatever food you can manage."

"Don't we have cameras around?" Rabbit said, running his hand through his hair. "There are like, eight of them hanging off of town hall. Go up to one of them and ask for food."

I didn't know how to tell Rabbit about the storeroom. Because I couldn't. Because he would be one of the first people to abuse it. "I don't want those fuckers here again," I said. Rabbit would buy that. *He hates guards.*

He smiled. "Killing that guy really got to you, huh?" he said. "I'll see what I can do. I'll let you know tomorrow. Though, for the record, I am down to kill some motherfuckers."

I must have looked upset, because Rabbit kicked his foot at my leg. "How bad is it?" he asked.

"Two weeks," I said. "That's George's best guess."

Rabbit nodded. "You wouldn't make it three days in without a full-blown riot. Chances are, those chickens are first on the list." Rabbit looked up at the ceiling like he was thinking. "I got an idea."

"Yeah?"

"Yeah."

I frowned. "No, I meant tell me the idea."

"Oh," Rabbit said. "No."

◆

The next morning, I woke up to find Rabbit laying on my couch, tossing a ball up and down. "What are you doing here?" I asked, going into the kitchen and grabbing a cup.

"I got news," he said, setting the ball down on the coffee table and sitting up. "You know, you're not so pretty first thing in the morning."

I ran the sink and got some water. "If this isn't good news, I'm going to kill you. And where did you find that ball?"

Rabbit smiled. "Of course its good news," he said, taking a second to point to his smiling face, "Can't you tell?"

I focused my sleepy eyes on him. "You're high."

He smiled a little wider. "And you've got food."

"If I didn't hate you, I would kiss you," I said setting down the cup and walking around to the living room. "Where?"

"You don't hate me, and town hall," he said, standing up. "I'll race you."

"It's *alone* in town hall?" I asked, suddenly awake. I went to the front door and started to put on my shoes. "Rabbit, you fucking idiot, there's going to be a riot if they find it, we'll never—"

"Calm down," Rabbit laughed. "If I want to throw a riot, it would be way more fun than that. I have some Pinks watching it. Including Pitt."

I let out a long breath. "I swear to god, I'm going to kill you one day."

"Not if I kill you first," he smiled.

True to his word, the town hall was filled with boxes of freeze-dried food. Enough for three weeks, I guessed. Maybe more, if we skipped eating for a few days. I glanced up at the stage. The blanket was still there, covering the storeroom door. *So this is all new then*, I thought. *I wonder how they got it here.*

Every Pink we had left was there, standing in between the boxes and the growing crowd. I found Pitt easy enough, he was right in front. "What about the farm?" I asked him.

"Good fucking morning," he snapped. "I've got bigger issues right now. What are we doing about this?"

I looked back at the crowd. Probably half the prison was there, waiting. Pushing. "Fuck, right," I said, looking around. "Um, keep the Pinks here. Form two lines, one packet per person. Two meals a day, breakfast and dinner."

"All of the Pinks? We need to sleep, Heather," Pittman snapped. I actually looked at him for a second. He had heavy bags under his eyes, and he looked pissed. I had seen Pitt pissed before, but never at me. I was suddenly aware of how much bigger he was than me.

"Listen, I'll think of something. Just—keep everyone here for now and start feeding people. I have to go watch the farm," I said as I started to turn around and run through the crowd.

The farm was fine, completely untouched. George and a handful of Green's were standing with the animals. I hopped the fence and practically fell over myself to get to them. "Hey, I need you," I said to George.

"Go look for weeds, like we talked about," he said to the other Greens. They wandered away. "What's up? Is this about the food?"

"Yeah, can we have Green's watch the farm?" I huffed. I hadn't realized how out of breath I was. I felt like my heart was beating too fast, like my body was vibrating. "Can we?"

"For how long? We aren't like the Pinks, we aren't big," George said.

"Just until we get some food ready," I practically begged.

"That's a long time," George reminded me.

"I need Pink's guarding the food," I said. I looked back behind me, expecting someone to be there, but no one was.

"Heather, I don't know, Green isn't big on fighting," he said, looking around as well. "Plus, if half of us leave to chase some guy down, the animals—I don't know."

"Just for today?" I begged. "I'll work something out."

"Alright, I guess. Just for today though," George reluctantly agreed.

I kissed his cheek. "Thank you, you're the best!"

I took off running towards Delany's house. "Delany!" I yelled, trying the front door. She hadn't locked it. I went in and yelled her name again.

"What?"

It came from her bedroom. I started to walk towards it, then stopped. "Is Laura here?"

"No."

"Are you wearing clothes?"

"Yes! What the fuck is wrong with you?" Her door opened, and Delany came out. "What the fuck?" Her hair was half sticking up, half matted to her head. Had I not been so frantic, I would have laughed.

"Had to check," I said quickly. "Look, I need your help, I—"

"Alright, first," she said, pushing past me. She went towards the kitchen. "Calm the fuck down. You're being too much." She turned on the kitchen sink and stuck her whole head under, drinking. I took a few deep breaths, but I still felt my mind racing. Delany pulled her head back up and cut off the sink. "Second of all, I'm not in charge," Delany said, jumping up to sit on the kitchen counter. "So whatever this is, it's not my problem."

"A riot will be your problem," I said, making an effort to speak slower.

"A riot could be fun," she said, looking at me. "Riots bring about new world orders, you know. Set things right."

"Delany, I don't fucking have time for this," I yelled. "I need the names of Reds you trust."

"Why?"

"I need them to help guard food and the farm."

Delany looked me up and down. "Reds that trust me, or trust you?"

"Whichever is easier," I said. I knew I was speaking quickly, probably too quickly. I felt like I was going a hundred miles a minute. "Just someone."

Delany rattled off a few names. "And Socks," she said. "Leave him with the freeze-dried shit. He's not much of a runner."

"Thank you," I said, and turned off and stormed back out of the house.

It took me all day, but I got it set up. Half the Pinks were with the food, the other half with the farm. I had five Reds with the food and five with the farm. Just enough to keep things running. Come night, I would stay with the food and Socks would stay with the farm. Hopefully, that would be enough.

Sitting up all night and watching over boxes wasn't exactly my idea of an exciting night, but it passed without incident. When the Pinks and Reds started to come, I left it to them. I could hear my bed screaming my name, my tired eyes looked for my little house on the end of the block.

I walked through Red and saw people standing around, talking. "Foods ready," I said to a few of them. "Then work. Come on."

"Yeah, okay," they scoffed.

I walked all the way through Red. More of the same. I walked until I was in Orange. More people, standing around. Talking. Throwing balls around. Laughing.

I walked to the farm. George was there with three Greens. "Where is everyone else?" I called out to him. He shrugged at me. "Motherfucker."

I ran into Socks on my way back to the town hall. "How was your night? As boring as mine?" he asked.

"Fucking no one is fucking doing anything!" I yelled. People walking by us looked at me.

"What does that even mean?" Socks asked me at an appropriate volume.

"No one is doing the jobs they were assigned," I whined. "There's like, four Greens at the farm. I have ten people there. Red, Orange, and Yellow are all just standing around."

"It's early," Socks reminded me. "Look, let's go to town hall, get out food, eat, and then we'll see what everyone is up to, okay?"

That sounded like a solid plan, so I agreed. I was also starving, which made it all the more convincing. All of the Pinks and Reds I had asked to be there were there, which was an encouraging sign. Socks and I waited in line, silently. We were both too tired to bother.

Once we got our food, he insisted we eat together, talk things over. I went back to his house. It was the same set up as mine, but he had already made a mess of it. *Boys*, I thought. It looked like he had just flung clothes everywhere.

"Yeah, I'm sort of a slob," Socks admitted. "Give me that, I'll 'cook'." I handed him my packet of freeze-dried eggs.

"God, I'm fucking tired," I said, going and sitting down on his couch. "Can I just sleep and let someone else figure it out?"

"Do you really want someone else doing this?" Socks asked me.

"No, but I don't fucking want to do it either." I ran my hand through my hair, trying to get out some of the tangles. "What if I'm right and no one is pulling their weight?"

"Well," Socks said, turning and looking at me from the kitchen. "Not no one. Pitt and George are. All those Pinks and Reds are. You are."

"Yeah, but we aren't enough to run the whole prison," I said. "What about everyone else?" Socks didn't have an answer for that. "I should talk to Delany. She's good at this sort of thing."

"Delany used to light people on fire," Socks reminded me.

"Yeah, and we both let her," I reminded him. "Besides, she didn't want to. There wasn't exactly a lot of options."

"Well, what is Delany going to say?" Socks asked me. He took the water off the stove. "She'll either tell you to fuck off, let her be in charge, or what?"

I thought for a second. "She'll tell me to let them starve. Only feed people who deserve it."

"And will that work?" Socks came over and handed me a bowl of eggs.

"I guess, but—No. People are just going to steal food. I don't have enough people to protect all of it from a full-blown riot," I said. "I can't just let them starve."

"Okay, how else can we motivate people?" Socks asked. He sat down next to me and started eating.

"I could wait them out. Hope they get bored and do the right thing," I suggested.

Socks shook his head. "You expect criminals to do the right thing? Look at Rabbit. He would rather die than be helpful."

"He *is* helpful," I said. "Just not in the traditional way. You have to trick him."

Socks nodded, "There we go. How do we trick people into being helpful?"

I thought for a second. "The guards," I said. "If I tell them the guards will come back if we don't take care of ourselves that might make them work."

Socks smiled. "The five of you came here first, right?"

"Yeah, me, Delany, Rabbit, Freddie, and Pitt."

"Did the Lieutenant say anything about it? This is easier if we don't have to ask Delany and Rabbit to lie."

"You think Pitt would lie for me?"

"He doesn't give a shit."

"True," I said. "The Lieutenant did say something, like the cameras were here in case we needed something."

"Good enough," Socks said. "Call a meeting, tell them the guards will come back and order us around. I think we all want that less than we want to work."

I nodded. "Can I nap first?" I asked.

"Probably not."

"Fuck."

◆

"Listen up!" I yelled. The room slowly fell quiet. Aside from the Pinks and Reds at the farm, everyone was in the town hall, listening to me. "I've got some news. The farm isn't ready to go yet, which is why we have this." I motioned to the boxes of food that took up the stage with me. "Which means we have food until the farm is ready."

I paused. "Now, I've noticed not everyone is jumping for joy now that we have jobs. Listen, I don't want jobs either. But Lieutenant Gomez, the one who took us here? She said that the cameras around here are to check in on us. So if stuff starts going to shit, they're going to come back here. I know none of us enjoyed the guards at 456. I don't want to work, but I sure as fuck don't want guards here."

There was a quick murmur. "Even if you aren't worried about guards, the fact of the matter is, we need shit. We need food and our houses and to not kill each other. Which means we have to do some work. Some of us had jobs in 917, and we kept that fucking place afloat. A little bit of work is all it's going to take."

Overall, I think they took the news well. I wasn't expecting perfect cooperation; they were a bunch of criminals after all. But if I could get most people working, that was good enough for me.

As everyone started to clear out, Rabbit jumped up on the stage. "What?" I asked him with a sigh.

"I'm having a party," he sang. "Wanna come by?"

"I didn't take well to your last party," I reminded him. "I blacked out and Delany punched me in the face."

"Yeah, she does that sometimes," he said, nodding along. "But this one will be fun."

I looked at the mass of people leaving the town hall. If nothing else, I should go and make sure they don't fuck anything up. "Yeah, alright," I said. "I'll be there. But if you start acting like an asshole—"

He tsked. "That's unfair, I'm always an asshole."

I looked at him. He smiled at me. "I won't ruin your little prison, don't worry." Rabbit hopped off the stage and pranced off, probably to get high. I rolled my neck, then hopped off the stage too.

If I closed my eyes, I would have been back in 917. The air was cleaner. I couldn't smell anything burning or the stench of sweat and mud, but the sound was the same. People banging out songs. Someone singing that same song about how the world is fucked. People laughing and shouting and running and having fun.

Maybe this is going to work out.

The party was in Yellow, as all good parties are. I wandered around, saying hello to people, talking about the riot at 456. Yes, I was sure the Warden was dead. No, I don't know how. Yeah, I think he's an asshole. No, I don't know why they put us in this prison.

It didn't take long for me to run into Delany and Laura. "I thought you didn't go to parties," I told her. Delany rolled her eyes at me.

"I have no responsibilities anymore," she said. "Plus, someone has to keep an eye on Rabbit."

"That's why I'm here," I said.

Delany laughed a truly genuine laugh. "I would love to see you try to fight him."

"He's always high, I think I'll be alright," I said. "Have you seen him?"

Laura pointed back towards the middle of Yellow. "He was over there, arguing with someone about pricing."

"Thanks," I said, and started to walk away. Laura caught me by the arm.

"Be careful, it didn't sound like it was going well," she said, then let go of my arm. I looked at her for a second, confused, before I walked off.

If there was an argument, it was over by the time I got there. Rabbit saw me and yelled. "Our fearless leader!" he said, putting his arm around me. "I'm so happy you're here!"

"You okay?" I asked him. He was leaning most of his weight on me.

"Peachy-fucking-keen," he said. "You know, you're kinda stupid."

"What?" I asked.

"I told you about your aunt, and you never asked me again. Like, I don't care if you don't care, but come on," Rabbit said with a shrug.

"Alright," I said, figuring this was going to turn into some kind of trap, or at the very least, some kind of negotiation. "What did you find out?"

Rabbit smiled. "Nothing good. She got picked up for possession, served three years, got out. She went to a real prison, not one like us. She's up in Washington or something now. When was the last time you talked to her?"

I thought for a second. "It's been years. My mom and her had a falling out over—probably her getting arrested," I said. "Why did you tell me that?"

Rabbit paused to lick his lips for a second. "You're kind of a pain in the ass, but you didn't hesitate when it came to the Warden." Rabbit let go of me and spun in a circle. "I'm going to kill some more guards!"

"Excuse me?"

"I'm going to start a riot and get them here, then we're going to kill more of those fuckers." He grabbed me by the face, holding me so close I could smell his breath. "Those fuckers who did this to us. To *you*. I'm going to kill them."

I put my hands over his hands, still resting on my face. "Rabbit, you can't do that."

"Why not? They deserve to die."

"They are just guards. Just doing their jobs."

"I'm pretty sure there were some Nazis that said the same thing," Rabbit said. "But I see your point." He let go of me, suddenly, jumping a few feet away from me, then turning back to look at me.

"You have to kill the head," he said. "Cut the tail of a snake, it'll bite you. Cut of its head, and—" Rabbit banged two closed fists together, then let his hands fall like dust. "It's dead."

I understood what he meant. I even agreed with what he meant. It wasn't a good feeling. "Rabbit, you know—"

"Fuck them!"

Rabbit jumped towards me again, reaching out for my hands. I didn't let him grab me, so he started spinning around in a circle. "Fuck the guards!" he screamed, and people around him chimed in. "Fuck the guards! Fuck the guards!" he chanted over and over.

Pittman caught my eye from across the way. He nodded, and I walked around Rabbit and his circles. "Hey," I said, turning to look at Rabbit for a second. "He's such a pain in the ass."

"Yeah, sometimes murder will do that to you," Pittman said. "Want me to keep an eye on him?"

I thought for a second. "I don't think he's serious about it, but yeah, could you? I have to go home before I pass out. Don't look at me like that, I didn't take anything. I'm tired."

Pittman smiled a little. "George is getting me some stuff, but I'll keep an eye on jackass over here. Get some sleep."

I walked away from the party, letting its loud cheering and fighting and music fade away. It didn't take me long to get back to Red, where it was a little quieter. I went to my house and sat on the front steps for a second, just taking it all in.

My arms were resting on my knees, and I caught sight of the tattoo on my arm. 982642. I had never paid much attention to it. Everyone had one—except for Delany—in the same spot on their arm.

My mom hated tattoos. I could practically see her, sitting in her parked car, hands on the steering wheel, holding it so tight that her suburban housewife knuckles went white. "I just don't get why they do it." I could still remember her voice perfectly. "Ruin themselves like that."

I ran my hand over the numbers, then put my hand over it. That's who I was. 982642. Tattoos were not acceptable in society. They were the easiest way to tell if someone was "other".

I thought about my mom. If she knew where I was, what happened to me. She probably didn't. That was for the best. I couldn't imagine her walking down the street, people whispering about her baby being in prison. Good little Heather, the criminal. It would break her heart.

As much as I missed her, something in me realized she was better off without me now. I was branded—literally—as a criminal. I couldn't go back to her world now. This was it for me. This prison, with these people.

As much as I fucking hated it, and them, they got it. Rabbit embraced it. We had gone through the same shit. How could I explain to my mother the casual mass grave? How I had to pee next to cages were we burned people alive? She would think I was a monster.

I wanted a normal life, to go to school and have a job, get married and maybe have a kid or two, but that was taken from me. I was going to mourn it. I could feel the sadness around my heart already, squeezing it like a boa constrictor. But I could also hear the party in the distance. Those were my people now. It made my heart hurt a little less. I wondered if anyone here could do tattoos.

◆

I woke up the next day to the sun in my eyes. I rolled over and pulled the covers up under my chin. My eyes were still heavy, only half opened. Something in my body screamed at me to stay exactly where I was. I felt like someone was watching me.

I lifted my head just enough to look around the little room. There was no one there, no immediate danger. I don't know why I had this gut feeling that I should stay in bed. But I did. I laid there, thinking.

I wondered about Lieutenant Gomez. She seemed nice. I wonder if she really was. I wondered if she actually would help us. I wondered if anyone would.

We want you all to be happy. I could hear her voice, clear as day.

Happy. I didn't even know what would make me happy. Nothing. There was nothing that could make this better, undo what I had gone through, put me back to where I was before this. Nothing.

Happy. I couldn't even say the word. *Happy.* It felt so distant, not even a memory, but a grainy old home video, something I wanted to remember, but all I had was the video. *Happy.*

When was the last time I was happy?

I could see myself, sitting on my couch, reading. I used to read a lot. A lot of different books, but I always liked them. I would read for hours. I could see myself running. Not the panicked kind of run I did now, only when it was worth the effort. Just running, for fun, with friends. I could see myself riding my bike, petting a dog, laughing, eating ice cream.

All of that seemed so impossibly far away. When I saw my file at 456, I had only been in prison for a few months. I don't think it had even been a year yet. Maybe I was close to a year, by now. I had no concept of time anymore. Maybe that's why my old life felt so far away.

When I first got to 917, it crossed my mind that maybe I had died and I was in hell, or worse, purgatory. Even though I knew that wasn't true, a part of me did die. And I got reincarnated into a shittier version of myself.

I don't know how long I laid in bed, musing over the life that I had lost. Musing isn't the right word. I was grieving. I had had grandparents pass, my old preschool teacher, pets. I have missed all of them, cried at their funerals, thought about my life without them. But my life did go on. I had never grieved over someone who was still alive. How do you properly mourn yourself?

I rolled around in bed, thinking. I had this odd feeling in my chest like I was going to cry, but nothing ever came. Someone knocked on my door, and I screamed down the hallway, asking what they wanted.

No one answered, so I went back to thinking about my friends, the dog next door, my pink painted room with press on stars on the ceiling. And the things I wouldn't have. A car, a movie date, a college degree.

I heard the front door open. Normally, that would have been enough to launch me from my bed. I didn't even lift my head. I could hear them walk down the hallway, I could hear their hand on the doorknob.

The door opened, and Rabbit was standing there, his hands on his hips. "What the fuck are you doing?" he asked me.

"Sleeping."

Rabbit looked at me.

"What do you want?" I asked him.

He shrugged. "No one has seen you. You aren't running around like a chicken without a head. I got curious," he said, looking around the room. "I was hoping you were holed up here with someone. You are always such a disappointment."

"To you and me both," I agreed.

Rabbit looked at me. "Get up," he said simply.

"I don't want to."

"I don't care what you want."

"Rabbit, go away."

"No. Get up."

"Why?"

"Because I said so."

"Rabbit—"

He cut me off by reaching over, grabbing the covers, and ripping them away. I gasped at the sudden cold air and scrambled to grab them back. When I reached out my arms, he grabbed me by the wrists and threw me towards him with such force, we were both thrown against the wall.

I pushed away from him, and he smiled. "Now that you're out of bed, come on," he said. "I want to show you something."

"I don't care," I said, reaching back for the bed.

Rabbit was always small; he had maybe four inches on me and was skinny as all hell. Nonetheless, he managed to grab me by the shoulder, spin me around, and threw me over his shoulder.

"Rabbit, put me down!" I screamed. This wasn't a cute, friendly scream. I was screaming like a maniac. "Put me down!"

I didn't kick or punch him, and ignoring my screams, he carried me out of the house and onto the street, where he basically just dropped me. I managed to land on my feet. "What the fuck is wrong with you?" I screamed at him. "Leave me the fuck alone!"

"No," Rabbit said. He didn't scream back at me. He spoke uncharacteristically calmly. He turned around, ran back into my house, and came back out with shoes. "Put these on."

"I'm not going anywhere with you," I yelled at him. He was holding my shoes out in front of me. I slapped them out of his hands.

He picked them up. "Take them."

I did. I took them and threw them back at him. "Leave me alone."

Rabbit moved so quickly, I hardly had time to realize what was happening. He grabbed me by the back of the head. He used his other hand to force something into my mouth, then put his hand over my mouth and nose until I swallowed, scratching at him and pulling at his hair.

"What the fuck?" I screamed when he let go of me. I took a few steps back from him and wiped my mouth off.

"Next time someone does that, go for their eyes," Rabbit said, almost annoyed. "It's like we have to teach you everything. Come on."

"No, what the fuck was that?" I asked, running my hand through my hair. I wanted to throw it up. I should have thrown it up. I don't know why I didn't. Shock, maybe? Looking back, I don't think I cared what it was.

"*Oh my god*, you ask so many questions," Rabbit said, throwing his head back to look at the sky. "Just come on," he groaned.

I don't know if it was what Rabbit gave me or just the general lack of willpower I felt to fight him anymore, but when he started to walk away, I shoved my feet in my shoes and followed him.

"See, things didn't fall apart without me," I snipped at we walked. It was late afternoon already. I had no idea how long I had laid in my bed.

"You're so bitchy when you're sad," he snipped back.

"Jokes on you, I'm always bitchy," I said.

Rabbit rolled his eyes. "Yeah, we get it, you're all tough and emo now. Shut up."

"If you're just going to be a dick to me, why do you even want to hang out with me?" I asked. We were walking through Yellow. There weren't too many people around. In my head, I thought they were off working, helping run my prison. I shouldn't have been so hopeful.

"Because you're just *so* pretty," Rabbit teased.

"Are you more annoying than usual today?" I asked.

"Well, I did throw you out of your house and drug you, so I'm going to go with yeah," Rabbit said. We were walking towards the field.

"Where are we—"

We moved past one of the houses and I saw everyone in the prison. There were so many people, it had to be everyone. For a second, my heart skipped a beat. *The food.* Then I realized it was dead silent. We were never silent. Instantly, all of the hair on my body stood on end. "What is this?" I whispered to Rabbit. He took my hand and led me into the crowd.

They parted as we moved. The grass was still growing in, only a few inches high. We were trampling it. Finally, we made it to the center.

It was Tiger.

He was there, on the ground. I had barely known him. His white skin looked blue. He was in Orange, one of Noel's friends. When the storm destroyed Red, he helped me find Delany. He was a nice kid, friendly. Everyone seemed to like him.

His skin looked cold. There was a thick and brown pool of blood under him, a dark red circle on his left side. His dark brown eyes were still open, his mouth as well. He looked shocked. I knelt down next to him. The side of his head looked like it had been cracked. His skin and hair looked crumbled in an unnatural way under a dried ocean of black blood.

I looked up at Rabbit. "What happened?" I whispered.

Rabbit shrugged. "Cassidy found him an hour ago."

I wanted to feel something. I knew I should have felt upset. I *wanted* to feel upset, disgusted, worried. Anything. But I had nothing.

I stood up. I realized they were waiting for me, all of them. I was supposed to do something, to say something. Their silence got to me. We had seen people burned alive, starve to death, get sick and slowly rot away. This was different. I think, like me, they thought we were different here. Better than that here.

What would Delany do? I looked around the circle until two Pinks stood out. "Take him to town hall," I said. I had wanted my voice to crack, to quiver, to show any kind of emotion. It didn't.

The stepped forward, and people moved out of their way. They picked him up—he was stiff. Carefully, the two of them moved Tiger out of the area.

The grass under him was almost black. I thought about asking someone to wash it away, but we had nothing bigger than a soup bowl to carry water in, and that wouldn't help.

"I'm going to get to the bottom of this," I said, loudly. "Try to get back to your day."

Everyone started to clear away, and the chatter began to pick up. I looked over at Rabbit. "Where's Cassidy?" I asked him.

"Oh, no. I'm not Pitt or Socks, I don't do things," he said. "Find her yourself."

"I figured you would be interested in a murder mystery," I said to him.

"I am," he said. "I've seen more dead bodies than you, so I'll be in town hall." He turned to walk away, and I grabbed his arm.

"Really, what did you give me?" I asked quietly.

"There's a dead kid being carried through your prison. I think you have bigger problems," Rabbit said. I didn't let go of him. "You'll be fine. I know what I'm doing."

"Your drugs killed like eight people," I reminded him.

"They were my drugs, but I didn't administer those doses," he said. "You'll be fine." He pulled his arm away from me, and I let him go, but not before reminding him he wasn't a doctor. Without looking back, he flipped me off.

I knew who would be hanging around when the crowd cleared, and sure enough, they were there. Delany, who looked slightly amused, with Laura clinging to her arm, Pitt and George hand in hand, and Socks.

"Fuck," I said. They all sort of nodded in agreement. "What the fuck?"

George spoke up first. "Tiger was a good kid," he said. "He didn't deserve this."

"Want me to find Cassidy?" Socks asked. My eyes drifted to Delany.

"Yeah, bring her to town hall. We should figure something out," I said. "With Tiger, I mean."

"And all of the food," Pittman said. "I know it's in packages, but still."

I sighed. "Yeah, that too." I looked at each of them. "Are we all on board for a murder mystery?"

"No, but I'm curious, so I'll hang," Delany said. "By the way, Tiger used drugs and Rabbit followed the body, so you might want to get over there."

"I don't care if Rabbit steals drugs off of a dead body," I said. I started to walk off, and they followed me.

"Unless he was killed over the drugs, in which case you need Rabbit not to swallow or snort them," Delany said. She was walking casually next to me, Laura in tow.

"Fuck," I groaned. I looked at Delany. She gave me a smirk, showing off that we both knew she was right. I took a deep breath, and went sprinting towards town hall.

When I got there, the two Pinks were still there. "Has Rabbit touched him?" I huffed. Rabbit, who was sitting on the stage a few feet from where they laid Tiger down, threw both hands up. I pointed at Rabbit. "Down."

Rabbit hopped down. "What did I do?" he asked, hands still up.

"You guys can go, thank you," I said to the two Pinks. They clearly wanted no part in what was going on, and hurried off. Once they were out earshot, I looked at Rabbit. "Did you sell Tiger anything?"

"Not since we got here," Rabbit said. I could never tell if he was being honest.

"Are you sure?" I asked again.

"Yeah, why? You think this was a drug thing?" Rabbit asked. "I mean, supply is more limited than before, but I'm not the only one getting shit in."

I wanted to ask how the fuck *anyone* was getting *anything* in, but Socks and Cassidy wandered in the room. "Hey," Socks announced. "I got Cass."

"Cassidy," she corrected.

Rabbit and I watched both of them walk towards us. The rest of the gang was only a few seconds behind them. Everyone met at the stage, looking at Tiger. It was silent for a few seconds before Cassidy spoke up.

"I can't believe he's gone," she said. "He was such a nice kid."

I turned to look at her. "What happened?"

Cassidy shrugged. "I was just walking around the field, you know? Like doing laps. Exercise is really good for you, you know, releases endorphins and stuff. So I was just kind of walking, and I saw him."

"And he was like this?" George asked. "Bloody and blue?"

Cassidy looked at him for a second. "He wasn't like, bleeding when I found him. I guess because his heart stopped or whatever. I guess he's a little more pale. It's been like two hours since I found him, I guess."

"Did you see anyone else?" Delany asked. "In the field, in Yellow, hanging around?"

Cassidy shook her head no. "I went and knocked on two doors, but no one answered. I saw TJ down the street and yelled for him, and he got Rabbit."

"Why did he get Rabbit?" Pittman asked.

"I'm leader of Yellow," Rabbit said, almost offended. "He died in Yellow."

"You aren't the leader of shit," Delany reminded him.

Rabbit huffed. "Whatever. I was a leader at one point and now I'm part of this little inner circle we got going on. Also, I fucking live in Yellow. I was the closest."

"And then?" I asked Rabbit, trying to keep everyone on track.

Rabbit continued. "I went and saw, got TJ to get Delany and Pitt, in the meantime, a crowd started to form. Once we were all there, we decided to get you. Which took forever."

"You didn't tell me someone was murdered," I said. "I would have been a lot more cooperative if you had." Delany reached over and slapped the back of Rabbit's head.

"Hit me again and I'll break your hand," Rabbit threatened. Delany said she would like to see him try. He went to stand up, and Pittman put his hand on his chest.

"No one has time for this," he said. "Someone just died."

"People die all the time," Rabbit mumbled.

"Okay!" I yelled. Everyone looked at me. "Let's fucking—Socks, go get TJ. Cassidy, go home." Cassidy looked at everyone for a second like she was going to say something, but she followed Socks out.

I closed my eyes and took a deep breath. I could feel—I don't know what it was. It wasn't my blood, but something else was racing through me. My brain felt like it was moving too fast. I opened my eyes and looked at Rabbit. "What?" I asked him.

"What?" he repeated.

"What—" I stopped. "Come outside." I reached over, grabbed his hand, and pulled him behind me. We stood in front of the town hall doors. No one was around, thankfully. "What did you give me?" I asked. "I feel—" I searched for the right word. "Fast."

Rabbit smiled. "Fast?" he repeated.

"Like I'm moving too fast, the—" I stopped midsentence to put two fingers on my neck to check my pulse. "No, like everyone else is moving too slow."

Rabbit didn't stop smiling, and I slapped his shoulder. "What did you give me?"

"It's a mix of shit, don't worry," he said. "If you get bad, I'll bring you down. We just need you focused."

"I'm not focused I'm—Cassidy said she found him all alone."

"Yeah?" Rabbit said. "And?"

"Tiger was down the street, but he's Green. Why was he in Yellow? Does he have friends there?" I asked. "Am I talking really fast? I feel like I'm talking really fast."

"You are, and you mean TJ, not Tiger."

"Did I said Tiger? I don't think I did."

Rabbit sighed. "You really gotta stop. TJ has a few friends in Yellow, I guess."

"Right. We should go back inside," I said. "If I get too weird, will—"

"Yes," Rabbit said, pushing me towards the door. "I'm not wasting drugs on you again if you're going to be like this. Murder or not."

When we came back inside, George jumped up. "I remembered something," he said.

"Cool, I know how to tie my shoes!" Rabbit exclaimed back.

Everyone ignored Rabbit. "What?" I asked George.

"TJ and Cassidy were a thing, when they first got to the prison, for like a few months," he said. I looked at Delany.

"I don't care who fucks who," she said. "But I'll take George's word for it."

"Alright, so what does that mean?" I asked out loud. I leaned on the stage next to Delany. "Either its really lucky that she found him first, or she went looking for him specially. Specifically. Either way."

"I would go look for Pitt if I just saw a dead body," George said.

"I would look for Pitt too," Rabbit agreed.

"No one asked you," Delany snapped.

"You would look for him too," Rabbit said. "We all would. He's a scary motherfucker."

"Yes, but that's not the point I was making," George said gently.

"I would look for Delany," Laura chirped.

"Shut the fuck up, all of you," I snapped. "Fuck. Let me think."

I could feel this ball of anger in my chest, right below my throat. It felt like I could have spit fire. I took in a deep breath. "We think Cassidy went looking for TJ specifically?" Everyone around me nodded. "He's not in Yellow, so maybe—" Before I could finish the thought, Socks and TJ walked in.

TJ looked a little pale. I wanted to ask him why he was so pale. Or why he had that look on his face. Rabbit piped up instead.
"Looking a little ghostly there, TJ," he said. TJ nodded. "Not good with dead bodies?"

It occurred to me that Tiger laying there, head bashed in and bloodied, and it still didn't bother me. Rabbit leaned on the stage next to me. I looked at him, and his bushy hair. I reached out to touch it, then stopped myself.

Murder, I reminded myself. *Someone just got murdered.*

"TJ, Cassidy told you about Tiger first?" I asked. He nodded. "And what happened?" He shrugged.

"Okay, you have to fucking say something, kid," Delany said. I realized the six of us, standing there, opposite him, must have been intimidating. It wasn't unlike the three men who judged me, before we got sent here. *God, I really hate that stupid rat-eyed fucker. I wonder what his name is. Maybe, if I ever get out of here, I could—*

"Are you going to bury him?" TJ asked.

"We'll burn that bridge when we get to it," Pittman said.

"No, it's we'll *cross* that bridge when we get to it," Laura corrected.

"It's a malaphor," Pittman said.

"*Metaphor*," Laura corrected again.

"You know, you don't need to be here," Rabbit said to Laura, as if reading my thoughts.

"Neither do you," Delany snapped.

"Okay, someone was just murdered, so if we could focus on—" George started to say, but Rabbit went and got in Delany's face.

"Really? You're going to be a bitch about this?" he yelled.

I jumped off the stage and got in between them. "I promise you two can bare knuckle box in the middle of the prison if you just fucking wait," I said. Rabbit backed down, jumping back up to sit on the stage. Delany went and put her arm around Laura.

"I don't know what that is, but I'll kick his ass," Delany said confidently. Rabbit opened his mouth, and I cut him off with a stiff no.

"So the murder," I said. "TJ, what did you see? What happened?"

TJ shrugged. "Cassidy came running over, told me Tiger was hurt. I ran over. He was dead. I mean, his head was all bashed in. I went and got Rabbit."

"And Cassidy?" Pittman asked.

"What about her?" TJ said. He shifted his weight.

"Was she upset, crying, screaming—anything?" George said.

TJ shrugged. "I mean, she was upset, I guess. Tiger and her weren't close, but she just walked up on him like that. It's scary shit."

George reached over and took Pittman's hand. I don't know what they were thinking, but I knew they were thinking the same thing. I made a mental note to ask once TJ left.

"Anything else? See anyone, hear anything? His head was bashed in over there, it would have been loud," Delany said. "Anything at all?"

TJ shrugged.

"God, you're fucking useless, huh?"

He shrugged again.

"Get out of here."

I should have been upset that Delany was giving orders, but as she spoke, Rabbit reached over and touched my shoulder. It wasn't until then that I realized I was rocking. "Okay," I said as TJ left. "What are we thinking?" I was looking at George and Pittman.

"Have you ever seen Cassidy not react to something in the most dramatic way possible?" George asked. "If she saw a dead body, she would scream. Instantly."

"Pretending you find the body of the person you just murdered is a good way to not be accused of the murder," Laura said. While she spoke, Rabbit mimed her.

"Knock it off," Delany growled. He mimed her too.

"Rabbit, you don't have to be here," I said. He was about to get up, but held my gaze for a second. "Wait, no, you do," I said, holding a hand up. He settled back down, looking very pleased with himself.

"The murder," George reminded everyone. Again.

"Right," I said. "So, we're all thinking Cassidy, right? But why?"

"Because she's a positive freak of nature who has somehow risen to the top of the food-chain while we were engaged in inter-tribal warfare, but has become too obvious and now we must band together to kill our common enemy?" Rabbit rattled off.

"Kill yourself," Delany said, almost politely.

"Kill me yourself, bitch," Rabbit snapped.

Before they could even move, I yelled for Pittman, who got in between them again.

"Someone was murdered!" George snapped. The room fell silent again.

I took a deep breath in. "Socks," I said. "You've been quiet."

He shrugged. "I don't know, I just don't see it. Yeah, she's freakishly nice, but I don't think she's a killer."

"What did she get locked up for?" Pittman asked. No one said anything.

"Cool," I said with a sigh. "Alright, let's give it a day. See if anyone else knows anything about her, why she's here, her and Tiger, anything."

"And him?" Laura asked, nodding towards Tiger.

"I guess we have to bury him, somehow," I said. Tiger wasn't particularly tall, but he was a decent sized kid. We didn't have any shovels or anything to dig with. I had no idea how we would manage digging a grave.

"We could just light him on fire," Rabbit suggested. "Viking funeral. Minus the water."

"We live in a grass field, dumbass," Delany said.

"Alright, fire can be Plan B," he snapped back. It was quiet for a second. Rabbit leaned over to Pittman and whispered. "Wanna know what the B stands for?"

"No," Pittman said.

Quietly, to himself, Rabbit whispered *"Bears."*

"What do we dig a grave with?" George asked. I wanted to kiss him. For keeping us on track, but also I had a weird feeling in my chest. Like my heart was trying to escape. It wasn't beating fast or anything, but I knew it wanted out. I had no idea what feeling it was.

"It's getting dark," I said. "We can deal with that tomorrow." I wanted to go home. I didn't care that Tiger was dead. I deeply and truly, in my heart of hearts, didn't care. And that scared me. I didn't want to be here anymore.

"He's going to be all gross and smelly by tomorrow," Laura said.

"Then you can go out in the middle of a pitch black field with a fork and dig a grave," I told her, a little more aggressively than I meant to.

"Fuck off," Delany snapped.

"You fuck off," I said, instantly regretting it. Pittman moved to get in between me and Delany.

"You know what," George said, "let's deal with this tomorrow, that's a good idea."

"We're going to have to serve breakfast with him in here," Pittman said.

"Carry him out by the fence and leave him. We'll dig a hole tomorrow," I said. "I'll figure something out."

"Will you?" Delany asked.

"Oh my fucking god, *leave*," I snapped. Had Pittman not been standing in between us, there would have been a fight. I wasn't even sure who would have started it at that point, but we would have fought. No doubt.

Delany and Laura left. Pittman and Socks carried the body outside, with George practically running circles around them, trying to help. That left me and Rabbit. We watched them leave together, just the two of us, sitting on the stage. "Can I be done now?" I asked him. When he looked confused, I continued: "You said if I got weird, you could fix it?"

"Oh, yeah," Rabbit said. "Come on."

We walked back to his house in silence. We went inside, and he told me to sit, pointing towards the couch. I did. He started looking around for something. "Why didn't you tell me Tiger died?" I asked him. He picked up a shirt, looked under it, then put it back down.

"What?" he asked, only half listening to me.

"Why didn't you tell me he was dead?"

Rabbit found what he was looking for—a bottle, the size of one of those old-school soda bottles. He came over and handed it to me. "Drink," he said. I smelled it. It smelled like nail polish remover. "Drink it," he said again, sitting in the chair across from me.

I took a sip. "Ew, is this—"

"Vodka," Rabbit finished. "Drink it."

I took another sip. "Do you have anything else?"

"Nope," Rabbit said. "I gave you an upper. You need a downer. Drink." He waited for me to drink all of it. I had had a few drinks in my life, but nothing straight like this. It burned.

I put the empty bottle on the coffee table. "Now will you tell me?"

Rabbit shrugged. "I wanted to make sure you weren't pulling a Delany."

"What?"

"Where you lock yourself away and be sad about your life," he said. "Like she did at the other prison. God, that was such a pain in the ass. If you refuse to lead, we have to get rid of you. If you're having a bad day, we can manage."

I nodded slowly. "So you drugged me," I said.

"Well, we all need a little help sometimes," Rabbit said. "Now get out, I want to go to sleep."

Delany was laying on my couch when I got home. "What?" I asked her as I kicked my shoes off by the door.

"What are you going to do with her?" Delany asked. She watched me take my shoes off, then watched me cross the living room and sit in my chair. "Are you going to kill her?"

"Kill her?" I asked. I was starting to feel better. Slower. More normal. "We don't even know if she did it."

"Yes, we do," Delany said, sitting up. "It's the only thing that makes sense."

"First of all, it doesn't make sense. She is objectively the nicest person here. I mean, also the most annoying, but whatever. Secondly, we have no proof," I said. "We can't just go around killing people because they *might* have killed someone."

Delany laid back down. "You're boring."

"I thought you were against killing people?" I asked.

"Innocent people," Delany corrected.

"Then why didn't you kill Rabbit? He killed Angel."

Delany didn't look at me. "I tried. Fucker is stronger than he looks."

We both knew she was lying. I looked around the room, my head spinning as I did. I had gone from normal to tipsy. "Are you sleeping here?" I asked. She nodded. I got up and took the flat sheet off of my bed. "Here," I said, putting it over her. "Good night."

I got into my bed and laid down. I looked at the ceiling, and took a deep breath in. *Happy*, I thought. *I'll show them fucking happy.*

◆

Time seemed to move at a weird pace. I felt like Tiger had just died, but it had been a whole week. Things sort of just fell into a routine. I wouldn't say there was any kind of pattern, or schedule, or any kind of true system. People woke up when they woke up, they worked when they wanted to, they partied when they wanted to. Some nights, it was loud until the sun started to come up. Other nights, it was dead silent before I even made dinner. I didn't care what anyone did as long as they worked. And most of the time, they did. Even if it was just the bare minimum. We were still eating freeze dried food, but we were eating. Things were mostly running well.

I hadn't thought about what Rabbit said at the party. I should have known better for a few reasons. The first being I knew who Rabbit was as a person, the second being we had been at this prison for a decent hunk of time, and there had not been a fight. At least not one serious enough that I knew about it. Knowing both of those things, I should have been patrolling the streets, waiting for something to happen.

Instead, I was sitting on my couch reading when I heard the first scream.

Naturally, I threw my book across the room and ran out of the house. I didn't even bother to put shoes on. Most people were running towards the screaming, which was quickly shifting towards cheering. Right by the front doors of the town hall, there was just a cluster of limbs and screaming and fists and cheering. Pittman was screaming at the Pinks to stay with the food. I pushed past the growing crowd.

It was almost like one of those cartoons, where two people fight and it just becomes a cloud of dust instead. It hadn't rained since we had been there, and the loose dirt was being kicked up as people fought. There were probably thirty people rolling around in the pile. It didn't take me long to see Rabbit's poof of hair.

Without really thinking about it, I jumped in after him. Luckily, he was close to the edge, sitting on some kid's chest, hitting him in the face, over and over again. I threw myself at him, knocking him to the side. We rolled, and I ended up on top of him.

Someone elbowed me in the back, but I ignored it. Rabbit reached up and grabbed a fist full of my hair, pulling my head down towards him. I punched him in the face, and he let go. I punched him again, and again.

The feeling of my fist hitting his face was so deliciously satisfying, I almost couldn't stop. I could hear someone calling my name, but it sounded far away. I punched him until the fight simmered down and was broken up, and everyone had calmed down. I could feel people watching me as I hit him one last time. His eyes were barely open, his nose and mouth were bleeding. Or maybe that was the blood from my hand. The second I stopped hitting him, my hand started throbbing.

"Fuck," I said, getting up off of him. I tucked my hand into my chest. "Fuck that hurts."

"That's what happens when you beat the shit out of someone." It was Delany. She was behind me, looming, like usual. She had blood on her hand, too, running down her arm. She noticed I was looking at it. "I cut my hand on some kid's tooth." Laura wandered next to her, but Delany didn't even look at her. "I want you to know, Rabbit let you do that."

I ignored her. Now that the fight was over, people were starting to run off. I'm assuming because they figured they would get in trouble. Which they would, whether they stuck around or not. As the place cleared out, Pittman walked over.

"Rabbit started it," he said, nodding at Rabbit, who was still laying on the ground. "Did you kill him?"

"He's fine," I said. "What were they fighting about?"

Pittman pointed up at the two cameras that were screwed into the roof of the town hall, pointed directly down at us. I rolled my eyes. "Can you carry him to my place?" I asked Pitt.

"Of course, m'lady," Pittman joked. "No food was taken, by the way."

I nodded. "Can you come too?" I asked Delany as Pittman scraped Rabbit off of the ground. Rabbit was completely dead weight, just flopping in Pittman's arms.

"You know how I love to yell at him," Delany said with a smile. Laura was still standing there. I didn't say anything to her, but when we all walked to my house, she tagged along.

"Put him on the couch—wait! Let me get a towel first, or he'll bleed on everything," I said. My little house seemed to overflow with four people in it, even if one of them wasn't standing. I fished out a towel and set it down on the couch. Pittman lowered Rabbit down.

"Hey," I said, standing near his head. "Asshole. Hey."

Delany lightly pushed me out of the way. "MOTHERFUCKER," she said in his ear. His eyes blinked a few times and he looked around.

"How long was I out?" he asked Delany, squinting at her.

"Like three minutes," she said. "Because you're dramatic."

"Fuck. You know how bad being unconscious is for you?" he said, reaching up and touching his head. "Fuck me."

"I'm sure all three of your existing brain cells are heartbroken," I said. "What the fuck was that fight about?"

"You're bleeding on your floor."

"Rabbit."

He smiled at me. I had known that Delany was right, that Rabbit didn't fight me back on purpose, but I had hoped I could ignore that fact and feel good about myself for a second. That I could feel tough for a few minutes. Rabbit's stupid fucking smile ruined all of that. I wanted to hit him again.

The door opened, and Socks appeared. "Oh, hey," he said, shocked. "I didn't know everyone was here. I wanted to make sure you were okay."

"She's bleeding," Rabbit said, pointing at me like a middle schooler ratting someone out.

"Shut up," Delany instructed. "We're good here, Socks."

Socks didn't move. I nodded, and he came in, squishing in next to Pittman.

"What was the fight about?" I asked again, bringing everyone's attention back to Rabbit.

Rabbit touched his head again. "God, Red, this really hurts." Delany and I both told him to shut up, then looked at each other. "I meant her," Rabbit said, vaguely pointing at me. "You didn't have to be such a bitch about it."

"Hey," Pittman said, and Rabbit rolled his eyes.

"Some Purples were being pains in the ass," Rabbit said, trying to sit up. He quickly settled back down. "You know how they are."

"Pains in the ass about what?" Socks asked.

"Just, stuff, you know," Rabbit said. "Is my interrogation over?"

I looked around the room. "No," I said. I needed—I wasn't sure what I needed. "Pitt, can you and Socks leave?" Both of them nodded and headed for the door. Delany tapped Laura, and she left too.

"Ah, the three amigos," Rabbit said, looking at us with a smile. "My girls." Delany slapped his forehead. "Fuck!" he cried, putting both hands to his head.

"What shit are you trying to pull?" she asked, closer to his face than she needed to be. "Why are you being such a pain in the ass?"

"Um, because of who I am as a person?" Rabbit said, as if it was obvious. Delany hit his forehead again. "Ow, fucking stop doing that!" he cried again. He held his head. "I don't like it here, okay? Fuck."

"You fought a bunch of Purple's because you don't want to be in a prison?" I asked him. "Are you fucking kidding me? You've been in prisons for years. Better answer, please."

"I don't like having a fucking job, or murders running around! I want to kill them," Rabbit yelled. "This place blows."

"You don't even do your job, and there have always been murders running around," I reminded him. "Stop complaining."

I couldn't help but feel for him, though. I wanted the DPWP dead too.

"If we can get them here, the guards I mean, we can—" Rabbit started to say, and I cut him off.

"Listen, I want to be clear. You are absolutely *not* killing guards," I said sternly. "No."

Rabbit nodded for a second. "You're right, we need to go after the head guys, whoever runs the place. Like the Warden."

"Rabbit," I said softly. Because I felt it too. The little ache in my chest that said *someone* had to pay for this. But we were trapped. Best to crush that hope now. We weren't going to get any kind of justice. Not here. "No."

We looked at each other for a second, eye to eye. I don't know what it was, but something unspoken happened, and Rabbit completely shifted gears.

"I don't want to work," Rabbit said. "That's not a thing I'm going to do. Ever."

Delany adjusted her weight. "He's got a point," she said. I had almost forgotten she was standing next to me.

I looked at her like she grew another head. "His point is that he's a lazy asshole!"

"I am," Rabbit agreed.

"Listen, some of us aren't good little worker ants," Delany said. "And there is a murderer running around. Which you have done nothing about, by the way."

"Bees," Rabbit corrected. "Though I guess worker ants are a thing too."

"We aren't going to work," Delany continued. "You've seen that."

I groaned. "We went over this. We have to keep the prison running or the guards will come back."

"And do what? Get killed?" Rabbit asked. "That doesn't sound so bad to me." Delany nodded in agreement.

"If you could have actually fought and killed guards by now, you would have," I said. "Just because you two are cool with dying doesn't mean everyone else is." The memory of Tiger, bloody in the grass, hit me. "I, believe it or not, am just starting to enjoy living again." I wasn't even sure I meant that.

"Then you can work," Delany said. "Let us with a death wish relax."

I looked at the two of them. "You just had to jump on his bandwagon, huh?" Delany looked at me. "You had to agree with him," I rephrased.

Delany shrugged. "He's a sloppy drug addict with no sense of right and wrong, but he's got a point."

I looked at her for a second. "You two aren't going to let this go, are you?" They both shook their heads no. I groaned again. I knew Rabbit picked that fight because he was bored. It's not like him or Delany had even pretended to do any work before. Bored people do stupid things.

"Alright, listen. I'll never admit that I said this, but if the two of you don't cause any problems, you can do whatever the fuck you want. Sleep with your girlfriend all day, sell drugs, whatever, just don't cause me any problems," I said. I wasn't making a good deal. They were already doing whatever they wanted.

Rabbit sat up. "Well, we're going to cause problems. I mean, *I* am. There's no way around it. It's who I am. But I can promise to try to limit my destruction's direct impact on you," he offered.

"Fuck it, whatever, good enough," I said. "No more fights."

"Will you settle for *less* fights?" Rabbit asked, sitting up on the couch.

"As few fights as humanly possible," I said.

"Define—"

"Rabbit."

"Yeah, yeah, yeah, I know, I'm a huge pain in the ass," he said with a smile. "I'll sell my drugs and try not to kill anyone. You don't need a second murder running around. Good?"

"Good. Now get out of my fucking house," I said. I looked at Delany as he went to the door. "And whatever nonsense you are going to pull in the future, because we both know you will, just, I don't know, don't make too big of a mess."

"I'm not planning on ruining your little community," Delany teased.

"Yeah, you are. Don't," I said. "And you can go too."

"Gladly," Delany said, and followed Rabbit out the door.

I went over to the couch and threw the bloody towel towards the kitchen sink, then sat on the couch. My hand was still throbbing.

The last hour of my life was completely pointless, but I didn't want to waste the energy trying to figure out the real reason Rabbit was picking fights. Might as well try to figure out how black holes worked.

Knock, knock, knock.

"Rabbit, I swear to fucking god—"

"It's Socks!"

"Come in."

Socks opened the door and closed it behind him. "You okay?" he asked.

I didn't know why, but I instantly started crying. "I'm sorry," I said, wiping my non-bloodied hand across my eyes. "I don't know why I'm doing this."

Socks went and sat down on the couch next to me. "Listen, it's going to be fine. Look," he said, while I wiped my eyes. "This is just like normal, adult life. Plus some extra bullshit."

"Some extra bullshit?" I cried. "I'm babysitting a drug addict and a feral girl, and I'm pretty sure Cassidy murdered someone in cold blood."

Socks shrugged a little. "Think of it as an unwanted pregnancy. You had twins, congrats," he joked. I was not amused. "Look, and the murder thing will solve itself. She'll do something stupid, and someone else will kill her, just like old times. The first month will suck, and then it'll work itself out. What do you think happened at 917?"

Socks got up and went to pick up the towel I had thrown. It landed on the floor, so he put it in the sink. "They didn't form groups right away, it was a free for all. Shit went south and a lot of people died.

Eventually, they made little gangs to keep themselves safe, then bigger gangs, then the groups started."

"If that's supposed to be inspiring, it's not," I said. Socks went into the bathroom. "That place was not exactly functional." He reappeared with a towel and handed it to me.

"No, but they didn't have a quarter of the shit we have, including you," he said. "Look, I'll leave you alone because I feel like I've done a lot of preaching lately, but seriously, don't worry so much." He gave me a half smile. "And think, maybe Rabbit and Delany will kill each other. Two less problems."

"I don't want them dead just— " I thought for the right way to say it, "—I need them to be less them."

"I'll go look for shooting stars and four-leaf clovers," Socks said, standing up. "Get some rest."

I must have nodded off on the couch, because I woke up to a soft knock on the door. The living room was completely dark, but Socks had left the light on in the bathroom, so when my eyes fluttered open, I could just barely see.

Another knock, and I carefully pulled the bloodied towel away from my arm, which was now caked in dried blood. I set it on the coffee table and went to the door.

"Who is it?" I asked. The door wasn't locked, but I figured I should know who I was about to let in.

"Lieutenant Gomez."

It was shock that made me whip the door open. And it was her, standing there, alone. "Can I come in?" she asked. I stepped out of her way and she ducked inside.

"What are you doing here?" I asked, reaching for the light switch, then thinking better of it.

"We saw the fight, and with the death—" her hands were wound together. "I was concerned."

"Are you scared for the prison, or of me?" I asked her, watching her hands twist. She stopped, dropping them down to her sides.

"Heather, I want you guys to do well here. I didn't exactly pick this job, and I know how the Department is. I want to make sure you're okay," she said. She sounded genuine.

"Why do you care? We're a bunch of criminals," I snapped. "Why did you come here?"

"To make sure—"

"No," I said, cutting her off. "If you wanted to make sure we were okay, you would have brought us here when the farm was fucking ready." My anger seemed to startle her. She took half a step away from me. I was standing between the door and her, and I could tell it was making her uncomfortable. I didn't move.

"We gave you the supply room," she said. "Why didn't you use it?"

I looked around the room as if someone else might have been there, listening. "We might need it later," I said. "I didn't want to blow all of our supplies now."

"But the farm—"

"A big storm, a fire, some fucking idiot tears through it; it might not always be there," I said, and before she could even say it, I added, "and the Department of Prisoner Welfare and Psychology might not either."

She nodded a little. "You don't trust us. That's fair."

"What is this, some kind of psychological evaluation some big shot wanted to add to my file? See how I'm handling Tiger dying? Rabbit starting fights?" I asked. "Get out of here."

"Heather—"

"Out."

She stood her ground. "Listen, I know they haven't been great to you. But we are trying to help. And I don't blame you for not trusting us. But hear me out. We want you to be happy." There it was again. *Happy.*

"I'll figure that out on my own, thanks," I said.

"Are you sure you can?"

No. But I didn't want her help. I didn't want their help. I didn't want anything from anyone. I wanted my life to be easier, for this to all go away.

"If you need me, please reach out. The cameras will pick it up," she said.

I wanted to know how she got in the prison, how no one saw her, why she even bothered. Instead, I stepped aside and let her leave. I locked the door behind her and closed my eyes.

A deep breath and I opened my eyes, picked up my bloody towel, turned off the bathroom light, and got into my bed.

Part Three

"Hey, Socks?"

Socks, who was standing in the middle of the farm, turned and looked at me. "Come here a second." Socks trotted over.

"What's up?" he asked, leaning on the fence. "You need something?"

"Who do we know that does tattoos?" I asked.

Socks' face scrunched up. "Tattoos? Ugh, I don't know, I guess Harper does some good work. Was it text, or a picture?" When I look confused, he said, "This is about Tiger, right?"

"Oh, no," I said, "Something else."

Socks smiled a little. "You want a tattoo?"

I hesitated a second. "Yeah, I think I do."

"Then yeah, hit up Harper in Blue. She's alright." Socks looked around. "Anything on Tiger yet?"

I shook my head. "I've spoken to a few people, but no one saw anything."

Socks grunted. "Well, let me know if you need me."

I had to ask around, but I found Harper in the field behind Blue, doing yoga. I waited until she saw me; I didn't want to interrupt.

"Hello there," she said, standing up. Harper was a pretty girl, blonde and tall. "Can I help you?"

"Um," I said. "Socks said you might be able to help me out with a tattoo?"

"This about Tiger or you?"

"Me."

"Figured you would care more about the murder, but sure, I can help you out," she said, walking over to me. "What do you want?"

"I don't know," I said, realizing I hadn't really thought this through.

"Well," Harper said. She didn't look like she was judging me, but her tone clearly meant she was, "How about you solve this murder thing we got going on, and I'll do it for free. Fair?"

"Fair," I agreed.

I wish I could have told her that I don't know what to do. I don't know how to solve a murder.

Instead, when she stuck out her hand, I shook it and walked away.

◆

"Hey, Heather, you got a second?"

I turned around to see Forty-Eight. He was a short kid but built like a brick. One of Freddie's favorites, when she needed something done for Blue.

"What's up, Forty?" I asked. He looked around, like he was nervous or something. "Everything okay?" I asked.

"Yeah, I just—" He stopped and sighed. "I think I know something."

"Okay," I said calmly. "Do you want to go to my house to talk about it?"

"No." The answer was quick and sharp. "I don't want to be the snitch," he said, a bit softer.

"Then tell me quickly," I said. We were standing off to the side of Red, right out in the open. He took my hand and pulled me towards the town hall, right up against the wall.

"Cassidy had been hanging out with Tiger a lot," he whispered. "He was really upset about Leah dying, you know, when we all got sick."

"Okay," I encouraged.

He looked around again. "You know Cassidy, she tries to cheer everyone up. A few nights before Tiger died, I heard him yelling at her."

"Why were you—" I stopped myself. "I honestly don't care. So you think they were fighting?"

"He was fighting with her," Forty-Eight said. "I didn't hear her at all."

"Okay, thanks," I said at full volume. "I'll make sure we work on the long food lines."

"Thank you," Forty said. He flashed a quick smile at me and walked off.

He walked off towards Blue, and I followed right behind him. "Forty!" I called ahead. He walked way faster than me. "Freddie?"

"Towards the left, she usually keeps the door open," he said.

"Thanks!"

I found Freddie sitting on her porch, cleaning her nails. "Do you do anything else?" I asked her.

"Sometimes you gotta scratch a bitch," Freddie said, looking up at me. "And with the current climate, that might be sooner rather than later."

"How much do you trust Forty-Eight?" I asked her, crossing my arms.

"Why?"

"Because I asked you."

Freddie looked back down at her nails. "He's alright. If he told you something, it's probably true."

"He's been bitching about long lines to get food, but no one else has said anything. I want to make sure he's not being dramatic," I lied.

Freddie shrugged. "Everyone has different perceptions. I haven't had a problem, but I go late. He usually isn't too dramatic, so take that as you will."

"Thanks, Freddie," I said and turned to walk away.

"Heather—" Freddie called after me, and I turned. "You're a shit ass liar."

◆

Cassidy was sitting in my living room, the six of us standing over her. Pittman was by the door, keeping an eye on the growing crowd. Rabbit bounced up and down next to me. Socks sat on the counter, eyes locked on the ground. Delany had her arms crossed on my other side.

"Cassidy," I said, "tell me what happened. Please."

Delany scoffed. "What are we doing? Good cop—" she pointed to me, "bad cop—" she pointed to herself, "and junky?" she asked, pointing to Rabbit. Cassidy just sat there. She had the sweetest look on her face.

"It's our natural roles, I think," Rabbit agreed.

"Cassidy," I repeated. "I want to help you."

The cute look left. "What's going to happen to me?" she asked, for once, her voice small.

"I don't know," I said honestly. Because I didn't.

She nodded. "I just wanted him to be happy."

"Okay," I said. "What happened?"

"Yeah, Red, about half the prison is out here," Pittman said, peeking out the window.

"I'll—" Delany said, then stopped herself. "He meant you."

I sighed. "We'll worry about that in a second." I turned back to Cassidy. "What happened? We found the bloody rock."

"I was walking," she started, "And I saw Tiger. He was crying. We got a fight a few days ago, and I went to apologize, but he didn't want to talk to me."

"And?" I encouraged.

"And, I— " Cassidy stopped herself. "You saw him."

"Well, fuck," Rabbit said as he stopped hopping.

"So, you admit you killed him?" Delany asked.

"Yes," Cassidy whispered.

"Heather, people are getting closer to the front door," Pittman said. "And they aren't selling cookies."

"What does that mean?" Delany asked me.

"It's bad," I said to her, then to Pittman, "Take Cassidy in the bedroom for a second." Cassidy stood up, and Pittman walked her into my bedroom. "What do we do?" I asked the room.

"We can't kill her," Socks said, hopping off the counter and joining up. "We can't."

"Old rules say someone would have to have actually seen her do it," Delany agreed.

"So we just let her walk?" I asked. "That isn't justice."

"Oh!" Rabbit cried, hopping from one foot to the other again. "We lock her up! Double prison! Prison 2.0! Prison Squared!"

"She killed him in cold blood," I said. "I mean, stabbed him then bashed his head in once he was on the ground." The bloodied rock she had used was sitting on my coffee table, now a dark brown color. A person named Alex found it out by the fence and brought it to me.

"How would we even kill her though?" Socks asked. "There's no humane way to do it."

"Stomp on her head," Delany said, her voice hard like ice. Rabbit wave her comment away.

"She didn't get caught stealing," he joked. "We should just Super-Prison her."

"Where?" Socks asked, sarcastically.

Rabbit didn't seem to notice that Socks wasn't being serious. He thought for about a second and a half. "What if we dig a pit and just put her in it?"

"We barely got a hole deep enough for Tiger," Delany said. She looked at me for a second. "I actually think I liked him better sober."

"If we just let her go—" Socks started to say, but Delany cut him off.

"She'll be murdered by everyone else. Then what do we do, kill them? She has friends, I assume, they'll go after her murderers, then we have a never-ending cycle," Delany said.

"We didn't have that at the old prison," I said, hopeful. I knew that wasn't a good reason, but I didn't like the idea of killing someone. I didn't know how I felt about Cassidy dying, but I knew I would feel a lot better if I didn't have to kill her myself.

"Yeah, because we had groups," Rabbit said. "I killed Angel for her crimes, no one killed me because all of Yellow would have gone after Red. I killed her fair and square."

Delany bit her cheek for a second. "Purple used to be a lot bigger," she said. "Until they tried revenge killing. Blue nearly wiped them before we managed a deal."

Rabbit smiled. "What a fun time that was," he said, clearly nostalgic.

"Okay, so our options are to kill her somehow, or lock her up somehow," I said. "Fucking perfect."

We were quiet for a few seconds, maybe ten seconds total. It was during those ten seconds that we heard a loud scream. "YOU STUPID BITCH!"

Delany was closest to my bedroom and ran right towards it. The three of us were right behind her.

Pittman was leaning against the edge of my bed, holding a growing red spot on his stomach. "That fucking cunt stabbed me!" he yelled, seemingly more shocked than angry. The only window had its shutters open.

"After her!" Rabbit yelled, then practically threw himself out the window. Delany and I looked at each other.

"Someone has to stop the bleeding," I said. Delany looked at Pitt.

"Someone has to catch her before the angry mob does," she said.

"And get George," Pittman added.

"And get George," Delany repeated.

Before I could give orders, Delany grabbed one of the pillows off my bed and handed it to Pitt. "Stop the bleeding," she ordered Pitt. "Go get George," she said to Socks. "You, come with me," she told me. Just like Rabbit, she hopped out the window.

I looked down at Pitt, who told me to go. Socks darted back through the house, I could hear the front door slam behind him. "You'll be okay," I told Pittman. He was bleeding all over everything. "You'll be fine." I wasn't sure if I was lying or not.

"Just kill her," Pittman ordered. "Go!"

Rabbit might have had a head start, but by the time I caught up to Delany in the field, Rabbit was headed back our way. "No one's seen her," he huffed as he ran up to us. "Fucking disappeared."

I thought for a second. "Tiger's grave," I said. "Did anyone—"

Before I could finish, Rabbit took off running. Delany and I followed after him. I couldn't help but think of a life in which I wasn't running after an armed murder. It seemed like an easier life.

The grass was long now, maybe half foot high. We ran through it, the edges of the grass catching on our jeans, making little whisk noises as we moved. We had buried Tiger back behind the farm, but it didn't take us long to cross the prison.

"I don't see her," Delany said as we got closer. We ran until I could see a dip in the grass.

"She's laying down!" I yelled. Somehow, the three of us ran faster.

Rabbit got there half a second before we did. He stopped dead in his tracks. "She's still got a knife," Rabbit said, holding out both arms like he was approaching a scared horse.

When I got closer, I could see her, lying face down on the ground. Both of her arms were tucked under her head, and her body silently heaved, like she was sobbing. In her right hand, I could make out a sharp piece of metal.

"Cassidy," I said softly. "Hey, look at me, come here." Whatever hard-ball approach they wanted before, Delany and Rabbit both stood back, letting me inch forward.

"I'm just trying to help," she cried into her arms. "I just want everyone to be happy."

"I know, I know," I said, kneeling down next to her. "I want everyone to be happy, too."

"We are so blessed," she said, rolling her head so she could look at me. "Even at 917, we had so much." *No*, I thought, but I let her go on. "We had a beautiful sky, nature—each other."

"I know," I said softly.

"And no one appreciates it," she cried, almost angrily. "No one. Everyone is sad and angry and they have no reason to be." I was sure either Rabbit or Delany would chime in and say something, but both of them were silent. "No one is happy and it's their own fault," Cassidy cried. "Just be *happy*."

"I know, Cassidy, I know," I said. "I tried to get everyone to like 456."

"Exactly!" Cassidy said so quickly, spit flung from her lips. "You get it."

"I do," I said softly. "Cassidy, can I have the metal?" She looked at her hand like she had forgotten she had it. She handed it to me. I had no idea where she had gotten it from. It still had some of Pittman's blood on it. "Good," I said, holding my hand away from her. "Thank you." She mumbled something I couldn't hear. "Cassidy, you know you're in trouble, right?"

"Yes," she whispered.

I looked back at Delany and Rabbit, who were both standing there like statues. They didn't even acknowledge I was looking at them. I was on my own.

"You should—" Cassidy started to say, then stopped.

"What, Cassidy?" I asked, but she didn't answer me.

Behind us, I could hear the beginnings of a mob. They knew Cassidy wasn't at my house anymore, and they were looking for her.

I would only have a minute or two before a very angry mob of people found us. Cassidy had killed Tiger, in cold blood. We all knew that; she admitted it to us. She stabbed Pittman. There was a very good chance she killed him, too. No one would stand for that. Tiger was popular, well liked. Pittman was quiet, but no one had a problem with him. And like Delany said, under the old rules, we could kill her now. We saw her attack Pittman, more or less.

For a second, I could see how it would play out. Just like Angel's death would have. A group of people, stomping and kicking and fighting and crushing her to death. I couldn't protect her from that.

A drop of Pittman's blood ran down the knife and onto my finger. It was still warm. *Maybe that's why she stabbed Pitt. So we had to kill her.*

"Cassidy," I said softly. Her light brown eyes looked up at me. "I'm sorry." She nodded like she understood. Or at least, that's what I wanted her nod to mean.

I wanted a lot of people dead. People I didn't have names for, people I had never seen. Killing the Warden, I didn't feel regret. Walking into his office, I knew I wouldn't regret it. This was different. This wasn't the clean cut, black-and-white justice. This was some iffy, gray sense of justice. I didn't like it.

I reached out, brushing her hair away from her neck. I knew in my heart I was going to regret this, but all I could see was the mob that would beat her to death. Surely, this was better. Right?

I took the sharp piece of metal and cut her across her exposed neck. Not a big cut, but it was deep. I hit her carotid artery, and blood flowed out of her like a waterfall. She gasped, trying to catch her breath, and shook. As she shook, I pet her hair, waiting for her to stop moving. I wasn't sure how long it took. I didn't look at her face. I looked off into the distance, through the fence, into the world I couldn't reach.

When she stopped moving, I wiped her blood off in the grass and stood up.

"We need another grave," Delany said. The two of them looked like they just came back to life in that instance.

"We need to check on Pitt first," Rabbit said. I carefully put the piece of metal in my pocket.

"Let's go check on Pittman."

Happy.

◆

Delany closed her eyes and rubbed her temples. "And where is she now?"

I sat on Delany's couch, looking up at her. My hand throbbed with a dull ache. "Tied up, at my house," I answered. It had been a long time since I felt like a child, but with Delany standing over me, it was hard not to.

"And what's your plan now?" She asked me.

I paused. "I don't know. Get you?"

It had all been a blur. Cassidy died. We saw Pittman, helped get him to his house. I fell asleep. There was a knock on my door. It was the Lieutenant. My hand hurt. I was at Delany's house.

My memory of the last few hours was like a poorly edited trailer for a bad movie.

Delany sighed. "Lieutenant Gomez shows up at your house, for an apparent second time—" The look on Delany's face let me know she really did *not* like that I didn't tell her about the Lieutenant showing up the first time. "And you knocked her out because?"

I was quiet for a second. "She annoys me."

Delany waited.

"She keeps trying to help, which is annoying, and she keeps asking me if I'm happy," I continued. "She asked me about Cassidy."

"So you knocked her out and tied her up."

"Yes."

Delany sighed again. "You're spending too much time with Rabbit. Come on, let's go." She headed towards the door, and I stood up to follow her.

"Where are we going?" I asked.

"Your house, idiot. She probably knows something. At the very least, we have to make sure she doesn't escape," Delany said, then walked out the door.

I followed after her. It was a bright night; the moon was full and I felt like we could see every star. It was too late for anyone to be awake, but I could hear a cricket in the distance. It was peaceful, for a second. We walked for maybe ten seconds when Rabbit appeared out of nowhere.

"There are my two leading ladies," he said, hopping into line with us. "Where are we headed?"

"Go away," Delany growled.

Rabbit looked at me. "Oh, come on," he whined. "I can keep a secret."

"I don't believe that even a little bit," Delany answered for us. "Go away."

"Rabbit, go home," I said.

He hopped in front of us, walking backward so he could watch us as he walked. "Listen, I can either sneak around, find out, and tell everyone, or you can tell me and I'll keep it a secret," Rabbit said.

Delany looked at me. "Fine," I said with a sigh. "You can come."

"Fuck yeah!" Rabbit sang. Delany hit his arm and told him to be quiet. "Fuck yeah!" he said again, in a whisper. "So, what are we doing?"

"We're going to Heather's house," Delany said. We were practically there. "And you *will* be quiet." Rabbit put his hand to his lips, twisting an imaginary key and throwing it over his shoulder.

"If only," I said.

When we got in the house, Lieutenant Gomez was where I left her; tied up on the floor. She was conscious now, looking up at us. The three of us looked back at her and the red spot on her face.

"So, ugh," Rabbit said, scratching his head. "Is this a kidnapping, or an execution? Like, what's the plan here, girls?"

Delany and I looked at each other. "Kidnapping," we said at the same time.

"For now," Delany finished. "Pick her up, I want her on the couch."

Rabbit looked at me. "First Cassidy, now kidnapping? We really are a terrible influence on you."

I went and grabbed one of the Lieutenant's arms. "Rabbit," I groaned when he didn't help. He grabbed her other arm and helped me move her to the couch. "Now what?" I asked Delany.

Delany seemed very pleased that she was in charge again. And for the first time in a while, I was more than happy to let her be. She reached over the coffee table and pulled the hand towel out of Lieutenant Gomez's mouth. "What are you doing here?" she asked, very softly.

"We saw you were having issues, with fights, with food, with Cassidy. I was worried," she said. She didn't seem panicked, or upset. I would have been. But maybe I just knew us better than she did.

"That's it?" Delany asked. "You are here out of some motherly concern? Who knows you're here."

"My squad, about five people," she said.

"And what happens when you don't go back to them?" Rabbit asked. He had moved into my chair, sitting sideways, kicking his feet.

"They'll come look for me," she said. She was looking at each of us as we spoke, very calmly. Rabbit looked her over.

"Hmm," Rabbit said. He twisted so he was sitting the right way in the chair, leaning over so he was really close to her. "How important are you?"

"What do you mean?" she asked.

"If you die, how pissed off will the head honchos be?" he rephrased. If that scared her, she didn't show it.

It didn't matter what the answer was. I knew where Rabbit was going with this.

"I'm the director's niece. He is testing me with this prison, to see if I can move into management," she whispered. "So, very pissed."

"And there, my beautiful butterflies," Rabbit said, leaning back in the chair. "Is our plan."

"What is?" I asked. Rabbit, instead of answering me, motioned to Delany. I didn't want them to be thinking what I was thinking. Good people didn't think what I was thinking.

Happy.

"We trade her for him," she said. "The director."

"The Director of the Department of Prisoner Welfare and Psychology? You think he'll trade himself for her?"

"She's family," Delany said with a shrug.

"So was—" I stopped myself. "I don't know." I looked at the Lieutenant. "Do you think he would trade himself for you?"

She thought for a second. "For himself, probably not."

"Of course she would say that," Rabbit said. "She doesn't want us to keep her."

I ignored him. "Why are you a guard?" I asked.

"I wanted to help people, to get criminals off the streets," she said, softly. She wouldn't make eye contact with any of us anymore. I don't know if it was because she was ashamed, or if she realize we might actually kill her.

"You do know two-thirds of this room have never been convicted, right?" Rabbit said, kicking his feet again. "Some shitty work you do, Ms. Gomez."

"We're doing good work. I mean, we were doing good work. There are complicated things, like the kids here weren't well, and we—" she said. "The Department does have some mistakes we need to correct."

"And what do you intend to do about that?" Delany asked, crossing her arms. I don't think anyone was expecting that question. Lieutenant Gomez just sort of looked at her.

"I tried," she said so quietly, I almost couldn't hear her.

"Better plan," I said, hardly even realizing I was speaking. "We let her go."

"Even better plan," Rabbit said, "We kill her and then you." Rabbit looked at me. I knew he was thinking what I was thinking. Gomez wasn't directly responsible for our suffering, just like the Warden wasn't. And we killed him.

"No, shut up," I said, "We let her go. She brings us back files on the Department. Then, we work off of that."

"If we let her go, she's not coming back," Delany said. "We just said we would kill her. She's not an idiot."

"No, but I think she really does care," I said. "Otherwise she wouldn't keep coming back here and harassing me. I mean, if anyone caught her sneaking in, she would get jumped. She might actually be trying to help. And knowledge is power."

"Okay, Ms. After-School-Special, calm down," Rabbit said. "We have a tried and true method of violence here, and we are not changing that now."

"I'm not saying *no* violence, I'm saying *informed* violence," I said. "We can't attack an enemy we don't know. We don't even know the director's name, or what he looks like. They could send any asshole in here."

That made them both pause.

"Good plan, but you just told her your plan," Delany said. "So now it won't work. Moron."

I looked at the Lieutenant. "I know I'm asking a lot."

"You are asking me to kill my uncle," she said. There was no fear in her eyes, no pity. Just soft brown eyes.

"I am," I said. "There is no other punishment for what he's done." She looked at me for a second. I think we were both trying to judge if we could trust the other. "Listen," I said, "Go read up on 917. That alone is enough to condemn him."

"Fuck, this one burned her baby cousin alive," Rabbit said, using his thumb to point to Delany. "And this one," he pointed to me, "Just stabbed a girl in the throat. And the girl she killed only killed one person. Well, two if Pitt dies. Your uncle, he's got—" Rabbit took a second to count on his fingers. "About eighty-nine deaths on his hands," Rabbit finished. "And those are just the people we had to burn."

Delany looked at me. "You sure about this? You are putting a lot of trust in her. And you don't make good deals."

I shrugged. "No idea," I said honestly. I realized I almost wanted her to never come back. Because I wanted to kill the director. I didn't know anything about him aside from the fact that he managed the prisons. But I wanted him dead. And that scared me.

I reached over, and untied the towels from the Lieutenant's hands. "Don't fuck me on this," I whispered to her.

I spent the next three days thinking of Delany's cousin, Michelle. She was the first person I watched Delany burn alive.

I wondered if there was an afterlife, if Michelle would forgive us. Could forgive us.

I thought about the other people we burned, the ones I didn't know. All the people before I got to 917. I asked the Lieutenant to kill her own uncle. I wanted justice, but was it? Was this a solution?

You can't bring them back, I told myself. *The dead are dead. Revenge or justice, it doesn't matter. They deserve to pay for what they did.*

Whatever moral delmea I was having was only made harder by the crushing weight of time passing. Three days. Still no Gomez.

I had no reason to trust the Lieutenant, really. I had no way to know she wouldn't come back with a bunch of guards and kill all of us, like they did with the kids before us. I had no idea what she was going to do.

Happy.

Something in me made me think she was alright. Maybe not a good person, but an alright one. Average. It was some kind of gut instinct, something my body could sense in her that I didn't feel in anyone else I had met from the Department.

I was just starting to think I was wrong when there was a knock at my door.

I opened the door, and there she was. Alone. Unarmed.

"You came back," I said, then moved out of her way so she could scurry inside. I wanted to hug her, but I stood there, my arms crossed.

"I came back," she repeated. She held out a handful of files. "I read about Prison 917, like you said." I took the files from her.

"And?" I asked.

She went and sat down on the couch. "And I want to hear it from you guys." I could see from the look on her face she had already made her mind up. She had that heavy look on her face. She had read about the prison. She knew.

I thought of my mother. If she had done what the Director had done, what would I do? Did I love her enough to let other people suffer? I thought of Michelle again. *No*, I thought. *I would do anything to make things right. Even if it meant killing my mom.*

I nodded. "Stay here, I'll get Delany and Rabbit." I set the files down on the coffee table. I wanted to take them with me. I was afraid once I left, they would disappear.

When I came back with the two of them in tow, Lieutenant Gomez was still there. Still alone. Still unarmed. "My god," Rabbit said, sitting down on the chair next to her. "You are dumber than you look." I reached and took the files back off the coffee table, hugging them to my chest.

"You wanted to talk to us? About 917?" Delany said, cutting to the chase. The Lieutenant nodded. "Anything specific?"

Delany and Rabbit talked for about two hours. About starving, about how the flu ran through the prison and killed sixteen kids, how Angel died, how Delany was lucky enough to have a baby cousin, and how she had to kill her.

I hadn't noticed until she went to wipe her eyes, but Lieutenant Gomez was crying. "That's about what I read," she said, her voice cracking just a little. "I'm sorry."

No one said anything. She should have been sorry.

"What's in the files?" Rabbit asked, nodding towards me. I handed him one. We started to read through them. Delany looked between the two of us, waiting for us to say something.

"Shit we already knew," Rabbit said, "There are a thousand prisons, they get worse as you go up—meaning there are kids more fucked than us—all experimental."

"The DPWP made the groups?" I said, looking at a report.

"No, we did," Delany said. "After all the fighting."

"No," I said, almost handing her the paper. I handed it to Rabbit instead. "The Department saw all the fighting and made groups for us."

"That's not true," Delany said, "I don't care what that paper says. My mom told me."

Rabbit pointed to a spot on the paper. "They used us to make the groups, 'blah, blah, blah, reinforced ideas that would lead to the creation of a gang-like system, inmates adapted to it quickly'. Doesn't say how they reinforced that, but," Rabbit let his voice trail off. "You're both right, calm down." Rabbit handed me back the report, and kept his hand out. I handed him another file.

Lieutenant Gomez waited while we took turns reading things out. How the Department knew about the flu, wanted to see if we could handle it ourselves. How they purposefully made the prison near bats with the S3R10 virus. How they watched us burn each other alive. Rabbit read out the total number of people who had died at the prison. It was over four thousand, over the course of thirty two years.

I finally closed the last file. "Well," I said. The room was silent.

"That is fucked," Rabbit said for everyone. "Basically they knew what a fucking mess they made, and decided to watch the dumpster fire burn."

"And occasionally throw some gas on it," I added.

"They are evil, that's not news," Delany said. "Now what?"

Everyone was looking at Lieutenant Gomez. "Does it make me a bad person if I let you kill him?" she asked quietly.

"Oh, sweetheart, we are not the bunch to be asking," Rabbit said, reaching out and putting his hand on her knee. "We're criminals."

"No," Delany said, swatting Rabbit's hand away from Gomez. "What he did was evil. The only thing you could do is put him in a prison, where he would also get killed."

Rabbit nodded. "We'd stomp on his head until he died."

Lieutenant Gomez looked at me. I bit my lip for a second. "I order the Warden of 456 shot," I admitted. Rabbit rolled his eyes. "I found out I was innocent, and I had him killed. He didn't even put me in 917, but he knew innocent kids were going there. Byrdie was six. She was innocent too. We burned her alive because she got attacked by a bat. Six years old."

The Lieutenant nodded. "What do you need me to do?"

◆

I stood in front of the entire prison, again. Delany and Rabbit were at my side, waiting. We were all waiting. The room was loud and noisy. The last of the freeze dried food was on the stage with us, shoved into a corner. It would only be a day or two before the farm was ready.

I didn't want to break up the party. I could see some Yellow's dancing. Two Green's were play fighting towards the back of the room. People were joking and laughing. There was a kind of peace in the room, something I hadn't felt in a while. Probably not since Tiger died.

Delany kicked at my heel. I took a deep breath.

"Hey!" I called, then whistled. The noise faded away, and everyone was looking at me. "I've got news. Good news."

I looked around the room. *Please, let this go well.*

"Who remembers the Department of Prisoner Welfare and Psychology? The assholes who put us in 917?" I asked, and there was a resounding boo. "Good, so you remember them. Now, listen. I know we aren't exactly team players here, but I really need everyone on board for this. If one single person fucks it up, it ruins the whole thing."

Someone yelled out for me to hurry up.

"The Director of the Department is going to be here in two days," I said, and the place went nuts. People shouting and booing, people yelling at me. Delany whistled behind me, and yelled at everyone to shut up.

"Thank you," I said to her, then address the crowd again. "Listen, his name is Thomas Arthur. We got him to come here as a 'thank you'—shut up! It's not a real thank you, assholes. We have a friend who has been showing him footage of us being nice and getting along. He thinks we've been rehabilitated. He's coming for a visit and we are going to formally thank him for what he's done."

Before anyone could react, Rabbit stepped forward. "I think you know how we thank people like Thomas Arthur," Rabbit said with a laugh. He started to shadow-box next to me, and the cheers started up again.

I put a hand out to stop him. "Listen, we all want this guy dead. And he will be. We have to act civil for two days, okay? Two days is all I'm asking. Put your grudges on hold, steal the extra food afterwards, okay? No drugs, no fighting."

Delany stepped forward as well. "This is important. If he catches us being monsters, he's never going to come here, and we'll never kill him." She paused. "And I *really* want to kill him."

Above the cheering, someone yelled out, asking how we were going to kill him.

Rabbit took that one. "This man," Rabbit said, very dramatically, "Stole our *time*. He stole our *childhoods*. Our *freedom*. What do we do when we catch someone stealing?"

Nothing any of us would have done would have stopped them from cheering.

Happy.

◆

Delany, Rabbit, myself, Pittman, Freddie, and George all stood in front of town hall, waiting. It had taken a lot to convince everyone to go along with our plan. They had to wait, all of them, until the moment was right. Getting a prison of tormented children to wait to kill their tormentor was not something I was confident in. But everyone had agreed to wait. So I had to trust that.

"And you trust these files were legit?" Pittman asked, for maybe the ninth time.

"Between what Delany and I know, yeah," Rabbit said. He wasn't sober, but he was as close as Rabbit could get without becoming a mess. I think that was a huge sign for people.

"Did they said anything about the kids before us that they killed?" Freddie asked.

"They were sick, apparently," Delany said. "Said it was more human to kill them than let them suffer."

"Humane," George corrected. "Do we have proof of that?"

"The Lieutenant said so," I said.

"And we trust her?" George asked.

"Egghhh," Rabbit said, holding two fingers about an inch apart. "A little."

"Enough to risk your lives," Delany joked. "Look."

We could see the car in the distance, kicking up dirt. "How close do you think they'll get?" Freddie asked.

"Are they going to turn off the fence?" George said, looking up at Pittman.

"I have no idea how they've been getting in," I answered.

It didn't take us long to find out. The car pulled up to the gate, and nothing happened. We waited. About five minutes after the car stopped, a helicopter flew over us and to the car. It was completely and totally silent.

"That's some military bullshit," Pittman said. "The militarization of the police is fucking nuts."

"One problem at a time, baby," George said. "One problem at a time."

We watched the silent helicopter fly over the gate, and stop at the car. A ladder went down, and four people climbed up a ladder. The helicopter flew over the gate, about halfway down the field, and the ladder dropped again. Four people climbed out and headed our way. The helicopter flew off, just as silently as it had come.

The six of us went to meet them.

It was clear who Thomas Arthur was right away. He was old. Maybe eighty years old. He walked slowly, his back slightly hunched. The skin on his face dragged down, like it had been pulled down by the weight his bad decisions. Next to him, Lieutenant Gomez stood at the ready. On either side of the two of them were two more guards.

We had said no guns, and they complied. No one looked armed. But the guards each had a cattle prod on their belts. *One problem at a time*, I said to myself.

"Thomas Arthur?" I said, and he nodded. I held out my hand. "Heather Barrnet. I was elected leader here. This is Delany Hugh, Jack Pidone, Paul Brown, George Katz, and Freddie Scotts." I shook his hand, then pointed to each person in turn.

"Rabbit," Rabbit corrected, pointing to himself. "Pittman," he said, pointing to Pitt.

"A pleasure to meet you," Thomas Arthur said with a nod. We started to walk back to the prison.

"We are so excited to have you here," I said. Next to me, Delany was so angry I could practically feel her radiating heat. "You have done such great work over the years."

"Yeah," Freddie agreed. "Everyone at 917 was a fucking mess, but you really turned us around. We have people farming now, and doing yoga. It's great."

I could have kissed Freddie.

"You know, drugs were a huge issue in my life, but I got clean in 456, and I've been rocking sober ever since," Rabbit lied. "Honest to god."

We made it to the front of town hall. "Can we give you a tour? I would love to show you how much we appreciate the new prison," I said.

"Of course, Ms. Barrnet," Thomas Arthur said, motioning for me to lead. And I did. He didn't seem happy to be here, but he didn't seem upset either. He just kind of plotted along with us.

I had asked everyone to act friendly, to smile. Some people did. Some people remained in their houses, doors shut tight. That was fine with me. A few people even stopped to say hello.

We went through all of the groups. The five of us talked about each group, and what they used to do. Delany refused to speak. It didn't bother me at all. If she opened her mouth, she was more likely to rip his throat out than say hello. We took him by the farm, and George talked about growth rate and the water supply. Pittman talked about Pink, and how they were acting as guards for the farm.

The Director followed us around, listening. He didn't say much. Maybe asked a question or two. I didn't see him as the mastermind behind all of this, who made these prisons, who let us suffer.

"Let's head back to town hall, I really want everyone to thank you together," I said, taking them inside. Socks was waiting by the door, and grabbed me as the others went in.

"I really don't like this plan. He's just a figurehead, one person. He's not the entire Department. It will still exist when he dies," Socks whispered.

"I know, you told me. A few times," I reminded him. "Please, do this for me."

"They are going to take this all way," Socks begged. "You know how important having supplies is."

I gently pulled my arm out of his hand. "Justice is more important to me," I whispered. "Can you go gather everyone?"

Socks sighed. "You can't eat justice," he reminded me before walking off.

The town hall filled instantly. Usually calling a meeting was like pulling teeth, but now it was easier than catching flies in honey. It couldn't have taken more than five minutes for the room to be packed.

The two guards stayed in the back, by the entrance. Lieutenant Gomez took the stage with me, Delany, Rabbit, and Thomas Arthur.

"Everyone," I said. For once, I didn't have to wait for them to be quiet. The room was practically silent. "This is Thomas Arthur, the man who helped us all get where we are today."

A cheer rose up, and Thomas Arthur put his hand up to silence them. "When I started this Department, what, sixty years ago, it was a vision. A vision of reform, of learning. We had such big goals. We wanted to take the worst of the worse, the real garbage of society. The people no one liked, no one understood, and break them down. You see, you have to break people down in order to build them back up. Not everyone can do it, mind you. A lot of people have perished in our goal. But you lot, you've done it."

Rabbit looked at me and grinned. Any reservation I had about who Thomas Arthur was left. He spoke like he was proud, like he had done good work.

"Now, we can never put you back into society," Thomas Arthur continued. "It's too great a risk. But, what we can do is offer you a full and fulfilling life right here. And it looks like you are all well on your way to that."

Delany caught my eye as well. Thomas Arthur meant what he said. I could tell from how he spoke, he really thought he had helped us. He thought he had made the world a better place by locking us up. Not just us, all the kids in all the prisons. The pride he had in his work was clear in his voice.

"I am just so happy our most intense prisons have been successful in their mission," Thomas Arthur said. "I am so pleased to see you all functioning here."

But I didn't care what his intentions were. I didn't care if he genuinely wanted the best for us, wanted us to be happy. Intentions don't matter when you get results like that.

The three of us stepped behind him. It happened so quickly, it felt like a dream. Each of us, with two hands, shoved with all our power. This frail, corrupt, evil, intolerable man tumbled forward and into the crowd.

It was like a group of piranhas. I couldn't even hear his screams over the cheers. The people in the back turned on the guards. After a few seconds of fighting, they had wrestled away the cattle prods and had knocked both guards out.

People were holding up bits of Thomas Arthur's clothing, fists full of his barely-there hair. I had learned in school, once, that people had lined up to spit on Mussolini's dead body. I'm sure we would line up to piss on Thomas Arthur's.

I had been worried about us getting out of hand, of killing the guards, or going after Lieutenant Gomez. No one did. With the guards knocked out and Thomas Arthur good and dead, a sort of parade followed, with everyone marching out of the town hall, holding up their trophies. It must have been less than a minute before it was all over.

As the celebration moved outside, I looked at Lieutenant Gomez. "You okay?" I asked her. She was looking straight up at the ceiling.

"I think if I look, I'll—" she searched for the word. "Melt."

I reached out and took her hand. "I'll lead you out."

I didn't look, either. For all the violence I had seen, I had never seen someone mobbed like that. But I had learned enough to know that I did not want to see Thomas Arthur now.

Once we were outside, she took her head down. "I hope—" she started to say, then stopped. "I think you all can move on now." The celebration was still going on, and rang out behind us like an exclamation point on her sentence.

"You did a hard thing," I said. "But you gave us a sense of justice."

"We're still plenty pissed," Rabbit clarified. "But not at you."

Delany nodded. "I'll never admit I said it, but you're good people."

"You might not realize it yet," Rabbit said, "But that's pretty much better than a Nobel Peace Prize."

The Lieutenant laughed. "I'll be sure to remember that." She looked back at the town hall for a second. "My guards?"

"I'll have Pitt and some Pink's carry them out to be picked up," I said. "I'm sure he's around here somewhere."

Lieutenant Gomez nodded. She held out her hand to me. I shook it.

Happy.

◆

Five months had passed. The grass over both of the graves behind the farm had grown back. There were a few rocks to mark where Tiger and Cassidy's heads were, nothing more.

I went to their graves a lot. There should have been more. One for Noel, for Rue, for Brock. For Byrdie, Angel, and Cye. But all we had were these two.

George and Pittman were walking towards me. Pittman was still walking with a bit of a limp, but George got him out and moving, trying to do some homemade kind of physical therapy. I watched the wind make the grass dance over their graves while I waited.

I ran my thumb over my new tattoo, right under my numbers;
Happy

"Hey," George said when they got close. They moved slowly, at Pittman's pace. "You still over here?"

"Yeah," I said, nodding towards the graves. "Seems like someone should be."

George nodded. "Cassidy was a good kid. I don't know what happened to her."

"That kind of blinding positivity can kill you," Pittman said.

"The world is a darker place without her," George said. "Without both of them."

I still wasn't sure if her death was justice. It didn't give me that sense of peace Thomas Arthur's death did, or the Wardens. Some people were beyond redemption. I wasn't sure about Cassidy.

"You're turning into quite the killer," Pittman said. When I didn't say anything, he nudged my shoulder. "No one deserves to die, but some people don't deserve to live, either."

"Come on," George said, holding out his arm, "I made a cheesecake."

"Cheesecake?" I said, taking his arm in mine. "How the fuck did you manage that?"

Made in the USA
Columbia, SC
26 August 2022